The Nothing Waltz

The Nothing Waltz

John Pigeau

Hidden Brook Press

First Edition

Hidden Brook Press
www.HiddenBrookPress.com
writers@HiddenBrookPress.com

The Nothing Waltz
by John Pigeau

Editor – Erin Daley
Cover Design – John Pigeau
Layout and Design – Richard M. Grove

Typeset in Garamond
Printed and bound in Canada

ONTARIO ARTS COUNCIL
CONSEIL DES ARTS DE L'ONTARIO

The author gratefully acknowledges the support of the Ontario Arts Council for a Writers' Works In Progress grant received during the writing of this book.

Library and Archives Canada Cataloguing in Publication

Pigeau, John, 1969-
The nothing waltz / by John Pigeau.

ISBN 978-1-897475-37-9

I. Title.

PS8631.I4758N68 2009 C813'.6 C2009-903774-2

For my mother and father
Anna and Ernie Pigeau
My sister Liz

and in memory of my grandparents
Lionel and Loretta Pigeau,
and my grandmother,
Lula Chapman.

The Nothing Waltz

Book One

The Orphan Diaries

EVEN BEFORE HIS MOTHER DIED far too young, Finny
McKee had been an exceptionally nervous child. For as long as
he could remember, Finny was riddled with anxiety; he was shy
and anxious and easily agitated. He was afraid of a great many
things, and not simply those things feared by most children, like
thunderstorms or the dark or creaky noises in the night. Finny's
list of fears was long, and some of them were irrational.

One such fear emerged when he was being potty trained.
Quite simply, Finny feared his heart would come out of his
bum. In fact, if he pushed hard enough, he reasoned as a
toddler, his entire insides would come bursting out of him.

"Don't be silly," his mother, Rosemary, soothed him, in her
soft, good-humoured tone. "That will never happen. It has
never happened to any little boy in all of history."

But Finny didn't find his mother's words very reassuring.
He wailed with horror every time he was placed on the potty.
Consequently, he was not properly toilet trained until he was six,
forcing him to miss both junior and senior kindergarten, and
begin school in grade one.

Yet another irrational fear arose one morning when Finny
was sitting at the breakfast table with his mother, incuriously
probing one of his ears with an index finger. When he saw the
waxy, yellow substance that came from his ear on his fingertip,
he began to scream in full voice. He believed, with great horror,
the yellow substance was brain matter, or maybe his ear drum!

Again, his mother patiently attempted to calm him.

"It's just ear wax, Finny," she told him. "That's why we

clean your ears out when you take a bath. It's nothing to be afraid of—it's perfectly normal. Hush now, sweetheart."

Tears streamed down Finny's plump baby cheeks. His face burned red and his golden-brown eyes grew large and suspicious, as he looked up at his mother's wide, pleasant face.

"You have to trust me, Finny. There is nothing wrong with you. Not one single thing. Everybody has ear wax," his mother told him. She wiped the tears from his cheeks with a Kleenex. Then she shook her head and looked at her son with sad, worried eyes. "My precious, fearful little boy," she said lovingly, half-smiling. "What are we going to do with you?"

But it was a question she could not answer. All she could do, she supposed, was reassure him, make him feel loved and safe, and hopefully his fears would dissipate in time. But they did not. In fact, Finny seemed to develop new fears nearly every day. One day he was afraid to brush his teeth, the next he refused to get under his covers because he thought his bed was filled with ants. He'd never been electrocuted, but was petrified of plugging anything—a toaster, a lamp, a radio—into an electrical outlet. Rosemary read several books about childhood fears, and she learned that children have more fears than adults, generally speaking, because children haven't experienced enough to adapt to or rationalize their fears. They needed to face their fears and given time, they would outgrow them. She hoped this were true.

Even at six years of age, however, Finny rationalized his fears, albeit simplistically. The possibility of being electrocuted existed and therefore he feared it. Ants, he'd once seen on television, travelled in hordes and sometimes nested in warm places like mattresses. As for brushing his teeth, he was afraid he might knock them out and swallow them. (He had nightmares, in fact, in which his teeth cracked and crumbled in his mouth, and he would spit them into his hands like chewed-up sesame seeds.) The trouble was, at six, Finny didn't know how to properly express his thoughts in words. Besides, he didn't want to complain constantly to his mother. He was an intelligent child; he sensed his mother sometimes grew weary of dealing with him, no matter how much she loved and doted on him.

It was true: Rosemary was a nervous soul herself, and Finny's sudden outbursts and nagging anxieties were difficult on her as well. She sighed perpetually and bit her fingernails to the quick. When she painted (she was a studio photographer; painting was a hobby), she nervously bit down on her paintbrush, tapped one foot, and tugged at her ear lobes until the *right* idea came to her. And like her fearful son, she rarely slept—both suffered from insomnia—and when she did, she slept restlessly, her head filled with uneasy dreams.

Often the only way she could quell Finny's fears and quiet him down, was to tuck him snugly into bed and read to him. The book that worked best was not a children's book, as you might expect—none of them captured Finny's attention for very long—but the dictionary. Finny's mother opened the family's thick, heavy *Webster's Dictionary* randomly and read from whatever page was before her. She had a kind, steady voice, and she read rather slowly, deliberately, like a well-meaning, bashful child: "Babble. To chatter idly and continuously. Babbler. Someone who chatters." She moved on to the next word, although it was true she sometimes skipped a word she could not pronounce. "Babe," she read. "An infant. An innocent or inexperienced person." When she came across a name, she often sounded intrigued. "Babington. Anthony, English conspirator executed for plotting to murder Queen Elizabeth the first ... in 1586 ... and to restore Roman Catholicism in

England. Hmm." She paused briefly, an interested look on her face. "The complicity of Mary Queen of Scots in the plot led to her execution ... in 1587. Hmm," she said again.

After she'd read a page or two, Finny was as calm as can be. Usually, though, he wanted his mother to continue, which she did without a fuss.

Finny's father, Patrick, read seldomly to the boy. They spent very little time together, in fact. Patrick was a very busy man, after all—the owner of McKee & Sons Department store, a large and extremely successful business established by Finny's great-grandfather, in 1886, when horses and buggies and streetcars filled Kingston's downtown streets. A tireless worker, Patrick (whose closest friends often called him Paddy) was at work more than he was home. After a ten- or twelve-hour day at the department store, he frequently spent late nights at Marshland Country Club, playing squash and tennis and golf, then later enjoying a Scotch and a cigar in the country club bar with his playing partners. It was often after midnight when he arrived home at the McKee's monstrosity of a house on King Street West.

Late at night, Finny recalled, his father would come into his room and sit on the edge of his bed, smelling of cologne and Scotch and cigar smoke. He'd ask Finny how his day at school was and Finny would typically respond with something vague, like, "All right" or "Not bad," and his father would say, "Glad to hear it. Sleep well, son," occasionally brushing Finny's cheek with a prickly kiss.

"Okay," Finny would say. Although he knew he would be up for hours and hours, hoping, even praying for sleep. By now he was mostly resigned to the fact that sleep would likely come only a few hours before dawn, and only then because of sheer exhaustion.

Like his mother's, Finny's dreams were uneasy. But he rarely dreamed because he rarely slept.

He would listen to the trees in the backyard, shivering, thrashing off one another, and losing their leaves in the stiff breeze off Lake Ontario. Then he would hear the floorboards creaking above him as his father went from room to room on the third floor, first splashing around in the washroom, cleaning up; then undressing in his bedroom and flicking off the light. And finally treading down the hall to his office, off to do more bookkeeping or budgeting, or whatever it was he did in his plantless, leather- and mahogany-appointed office.

Though they spent little time together, Finny loved his father. In Finny's eyes, his father was a larger-than-life figure, an invincible giant (he was six foot three, muscular, and fit), and a winner (he excelled at every sport he played). He was an articulate, handsome man with wavy black hair that gleamed in the sunshine and a smile so charming women often flushed in his presence. He was charismatic, witty and confident, but never cocky, which only seemed to add to his charm. Finny's only wish was that they spent more time together.

When he did find the time to spend with his son, Patrick took Finny boating (although Finny was afraid of the water, or more succinctly, of drowning) and brought him to the country club, where it was discovered Finny was an excellent golfer. He was a natural, much to his father's delight, with a fluid, elegant, effortless swing. By his ninth birthday, Finny was hitting drives nearly two hundred yards, outdistancing many of the country club's adult members. He was a brilliant putter, too, and soon became somewhat of a phenomenon at Marshland. Older members would stop in the midst of their own rounds to watch him on the greens, marveling at the boy's seemingly constitutional ability to sink any putt under thirty feet. Finny secretly relished the attention, but he relished his father's praise even more.

"You could turn pro one day, son," his father told him, tousling his son's curly hair. "Hell, I could turn pro if I had your short game."

While other children Finny's age were riding their bikes with friends, or playing baseball or soccer or street hockey, Finny could be found reading (he always had his nose buried in one book or another) or walking Marshland's lush green fairways with his father and his father's playing partners. Sometimes he was allowed to bring Fiona to the course; she was his best friend who also lived on King Street West. A piano prodigy, Fiona was a sweet, playful pip of a girl who talked incessantly and was prone to mood swings. On the golf course, she often had to be told to keep quiet while someone was about to hit a shot. (At such times, she sulked, but usually not for very long.) Patrick's playing partners thought she was a nuisance. Nonetheless, Patrick allowed Finny to bring her along as he believed—as did Rosemary—that Finny needed to spend more time with people his own age.

Also, it emerged, the golf course was the one place where Finny felt no fear whatsoever, like some people feel in the comfort of their church. And so when he turned ten, his father got him work at the country club, washing clubs and fetching range balls. Ten was, in Finny's father's words, "A suitable age for a boy to take on a part-time job."

Rosemary disagreed. "He's too young," she told her husband. "He can't even *legally* work—anywhere."

"Oh, nonsense, he's plenty old enough. Some kids have paper routes, Rosemary; Finny will be working at a golf course. Besides, all he has to do is pick up range balls and wash some golf clubs. Trust me: it'll do him a world of good to be outdoors, too. Plus he can open up a bank account and put away some money for ... well, whatever. College or a car or something else practical he'll want later on down the road. He'll be light years ahead of his friends."

"He doesn't really have that many friends," Rosemary pointed out. "He's only ten. Also, he's very timid."

"Well, he'll make friends at the country club," said Patrick. "There are plenty of other kids his age out there. You'll see— he'll have dozens of nice friends in no time."

To his mother's surprise, Finny very much enjoyed the job, especially because he could practice when no one was around. He felt a serenity among Marshland's rolling and luxuriously green hills unlike any he'd ever known. Sometimes, after work, he walked the course alone, with only a seven-iron and a putter. He found enormous gratification in the gentle game and broke eighty even then (he was a better golfer than most of the junior players, and many of the senior players, for that matter), but amid those tree-lined fairways he drew the most pleasure in the awesome peace that fell over him and emptied his mind of any disquiet. Never mind his score, the golf course became Finny's sanctuary.

His father was right too: Finny did make a few good friends, other boys around his age—sons of doctors and lawyers, judges and business people; he did need playing partners his own age, after all. Finny liked his new friends—his "golf buddies," as Fiona called them—although Fiona remained his closest friend.

By summer's end, Finny was so tanned from all his time outdoors, his father said—jokingly, of course—that Finny looked "like a foreigner." His light brown hair had turned a few shades lighter, and he was even a bit more confident in himself.

But something was wrong with his mother. Very suddenly,

after Labour Day, she fell ill. She complained of lightheadedness and a tightness in her chest. She took some aspirin and went to bed, lying very still as any sudden movement of her head sent her into a frightening dizzy spell. Patrick thought she ought to see the family doctor. But Rosemary said she just needed some rest. As a girl, she'd had a lot of inner ear troubles, infections and such; in time, they passed. She figured this would pass, too. But she was wrong, and on a sunny Sunday afternoon in mid-September, she died in her sleep.

She died of a "weak heart." That's all Finny and his sister, Maggie (two years his elder), were told; that's all their father would tell them, even after he knew the actual cause of death.

The McKees were overwhelmed with grief. Shocked and distraught, Patrick barely spoke. He seemed motionless. He sat silently in the kitchen, staring out the window overlooking the backyard for hours on end, not even so much as drumming his fingers on the table. He looked terrible. His face was unshaven and lacking in colour, and there were dark rings under his eyes. (In two weeks, his lustrous black hair would be threaded with thick strands of grey.) He allowed himself to cry, but only when he was alone; he felt he had to keep it together in front of the children.

Maggie wept inconsolably and was sent to stay with her Aunt Hilary (Patrick's only sister), in Westport, until funeral arrangements could be made.

Patrick called his brother, Jack, in Toronto and somberly told him the news. Jack, a bachelor at forty who ran a construction company, volunteered to drive down the next day and help with funeral arrangements and whatnot. Instead, he arrived later that night in his shiny silver Volvo, and began making arrangements at once. He also made the phone call Patrick hadn't the strength to—to North Bay, to Rosemary's mother. Amazingly, she was Rosemary's only family. (Rosemary's father had been a Norwegian soldier; that was all she'd ever known about him.) Sadie was shocked and deeply saddened, of course, as Jack told her the horrible news, but her voice remained steady and dignified. She would catch the first train to Ottawa come morning, she said, her voice beginning to tremble, and would be in Kingston by afternoon. Only near the end of the conversation with Jack, when she asked if Rosemary's passing had been peaceful, did she cry.

"She passed peacefully," Jack gently assured her. "In her sleep."

Sadie sniffled and a tiny cry escaped her, sounding like she said, "Oh." Then she said, "My sweet little girl." And then she began to cry in earnest, and noisily hung up the phone.

But Finny took his mother's death the hardest. He was traumatized. For days, he would not speak or drink or eat. He refused, in fact, to leave his bed altogether. He was pale and ill-looking and unresponsive when his father spoke to him. For hours at a time, he quietly cried and sucked his thumb.

The fact was that Finny was filled with tremendous fear because he thought, as any child might, that if his mother had a weak heart then he might too. He pictured his own heart bursting like a balloon, an image which frightened him so much that he trembled and barely slept; the sound of his own heartbeat kept him up at night.

Also, he could not fully appreciate that his mother had died. The voice inside his head said, *She is gone ... she is gone. Gone.* But he couldn't truly fathom that and he kept expecting her, at any moment, to stroll into his room and sit down on the edge of his bed, unfold the dictionary across her knees and read to him, lovingly, in her soothing manner. She would smile at him affectionately and the hairs on the back of his neck would stand on end, and he would feel warm all over, and calm and safe, as if wrapped up snugly in a cocoon. Now he closed off his mind to any other thoughts, shutting his eyes so tightly (because shutting his eyes might shut out any unwanted thoughts), he developed a nearly constant headache.

But eventually he did, in fact, sleep—though only for short spurts; a few hours at a time, maybe, though never much longer. Then he would jerk awake, his eyelids heavy, his vision blurred, his muscles tensed and achy—and he would remember where he was and what had happened, yet it didn't make any of it seem more real to him. His thoughts were blurred and muffled, ineffable, dreamlike. He also lost all sense of time. Days dragged on into seemingly unending nights. Sometimes Finny mistook twilight for dawn, although it hardly seemed to matter. Several days might have passed, or a week. Finny didn't know. Nor did he care. His thoughts were tangled up and trembling.

Then one morning, there was suddenly more noise in the house. Relatives began arriving. There were Finny's grandparents—Gram Bennett, and Grandpa and Grandma McKee—his Uncle Jack, and Uncle Ted and Aunt Hilary and their two teenaged daughters, Jody and Jennifer. Finny didn't wish to see any of them, and he disliked all the clatter: the chinking of dishes, the solemn conversations in hushed tones, the strange footfalls in the hall. The telephone rang at least three times an hour and the doorbell chimed just as much, as friends and neighbours stopped by to offer their condolences and drop off casseroles and trays of lasagna and the like. To drown out all the hubbub, Finny stuffed his ears with Kleenex. When his grandmothers looked in on him, separately, he pretended to be asleep. He wished he could make himself invisible.

The day of the funeral—a modest affair held in a small

Catholic chapel Rosemary had sporadically attended—Finny's Uncle Ted remained behind as a sort of baby-sitter. He watched television in the den, occasionally poking his head into Finny's room to make sure Finny was all right. Remarkably, Finny slept well that day. When he awoke, it was night time. Voices drifted up from downstairs. Without anyone noticing, Finny got up and went to the washroom. He drank two tall glasses of cold tap water, then quietly went back to bed.

The next day, the house was quiet again. It might have been a week day, because Maggie wasn't in her room but her bed was made. Had she gone back to school? Finny couldn't say. He tiptoed to the top of the staircase and peeked through the railing; he couldn't see anyone in the living room but he could hear his father speaking quietly on the telephone. He must have been in the kitchen. When Finny heard him hang up the phone, he soundlessly padded his way back to his bedroom, climbed into bed, and pulled his covers snugly up around his ears.

He closed his eyes and wished for sleep. Then he said a silent prayer of sorts to his mother, in case she might be able to hear him. *Mommy, I miss you*, Finny prayed. *I miss you, I miss you, I miss you, and I want you to come home. Please come home. I am afraid and I want you to read to me. I want to hug you and tell you I love you. I'll be a good boy. I don't know what I've done. I don't know why this is—why you are not here, Mommy. Why you had to die. I'm sorry, I'm sorry, I'm sorry, and I miss you so very much and I'll do anything and I love you, Mommy, and please come home.* He began to cry. Warm tears soaked his pillow. With the sleeve of his pajamas, he wiped his runny nose. He kept on crying until, eventually, it seemed he had no more tears to cry. His eyes burned, even his cheeks were sore. He was thoroughly exhausted. The furnace came on and began to purr. Finny liked the noise; it was comforting. He sucked his thumb and moaned softly, making a similar sound as the furnace. Soon after, without even trying, he fell into a deep, dreamless sleep.

~~~~~~

He woke up screaming. "MOMMY! MOMMY! MOMMY!" Finny screamed. He sat bolt upright in his bed in a cold sweat, his sheets soaked and his heart beating like mad.

Several minutes later, his father hurried into the room, eyes half open, his maroon bathrobe flying out behind him like a cape. His white pajamas were wrinkled, and the hair on one side of his head stood straight up. Finny's light was already on—as it had been for days—but his father stopped a moment and looked drowsily at the wall switch. Then he turned to Finny and said, "It's okay now, son. Everything's all right. I'm here, I'm here."

"My heart's going to *explode!*" Finny shrieked.

Patrick sat down on the edge of the bed and wiped the sweat from Finny's forehead with the sleeve of his bathrobe. "What? Don't be silly, Finny. Of course it won't."

"It will! It's going to *burst!*" The sound of his heartbeat thumped in Finny's ears. He shook his hands wildly in midair, as if shaking off water; he didn't know whether to clutch his chest or cover his ears. Finally, he hugged his chest and began to shiver.

"No, it won't, Finny. I promise you," his father said. "Okay? Do you hear me?"

But Finny's eyes were wide as saucers and his breathing was loud and rapid.

"Make it stop!" he pleaded.

"Okay, okay. Just breathe, son." Patrick rubbed Finny's
~~~~~~

back, making gentle circles with his palm. "Just breathe easy now. You just had a bad dream, is all—everything's all right. Lay back now."

Finny did as he was told—he fell back into bed.

"Take nice long deep breaths, in and out."

His father demonstrated. Finny tried to breathe like his father—his chest rising and falling, rising and falling, slowly, again and again—and after a minute or so, it seemed to work. At any rate, Finny was no longer gasping for air. His father was relieved. "Good," he said. "Good. Now I'll be right back." He went across the hall to the washroom and returned with a tall glass of water and a cold cloth for Finny's head. Patrick folded the cloth and padded his son's forehead. He couldn't think of much to say. "You should really drink some water, Finny. You'll get dehydrated. Would you like some water?"

Finny said nothing. He rolled over onto his right side and stared vacantly at his bedside lamp.

"How about a grilled cheese sandwich? You must be hungry. Or I can make anything you want. Just name it."

But again Finny did not speak. His father sighed.

It would be a long, exhausting night.

It occurred to Patrick, sitting in an oak rocker next to his son's bed later that night, that Finny's screams for his mother were the first words he'd uttered in days. Although Patrick couldn't decide if that was a good thing or a bad thing. His son was fearful, he knew, but he'd never seen him *hysterical*. It was unsettling, to say the least. Patrick felt helpless.

And sad. Dreadfully, profoundly sad.

Rosemary had been the one who'd helped Finny get to sleep. She must have had some sort of trick. Then he remembered: the dictionary. It was right above Finny's headboard, on a wall-mounted bookshelf. He got it down and flipped through it. He didn't bother asking Finny if he wanted to be read to—he simply started reading. Unlike Rosemary, Patrick chose his entries with care, logically. "Calm," he read. "An adjective. Of the sea. Still, without rough motion."

He glanced up. Finny continued staring at the bedside lamp. Patrick cleared his throat. "Of a person," he continued. "Unruffled, unexcited, unperturbed, especially when it would be unnatural not to be so. Calm as a noun. A period of serenity, a motionless undisturbed state. An ominous and uneasy peace. And the example they give," he added himself, "*is the calm before the storm.*"

He read to his son for another hour—*serenity, solace, soothing, placid, peace*—and for a time Finny closed his eyes, but it was clear he wasn't asleep. He scratched his nose, adjusted his pillow slightly, and once or twice, yawned prodigiously.

Patrick couldn't sleep either. When Finny's eyes were closed, Patrick ducked out of the room for a moment, went down the hall to his office, and selected a book of his own to read: John Steinbeck's *The Grapes Of Wrath*. But he found he absorbed little of what he read; the words looked small and trivial. He kept sighing, then developed a crick in his neck. He closed the book, leaned his head back against the chair, and rocked for a while. Dawn couldn't come soon enough.

But of course, it did.

Patrick must have slept. When he woke, he was bleary-eyed and startled, at first, to find himself in a rocking chair in Finny's room. It took him a moment to get his bearings. Sufficiently awake, he was pleased to see that Finny was sleeping, but he was alarmed by the sight of his son's face, which was such an unhealthy white hue it appeared nearly translucent. That decided him. Exasperated and sick with worry, Patrick strode down the hall, sat down at his desk, flipped through his Rolodex, and called the children's doctor's office. After three rings, a female receptionist answered, bright and cheerful on a Monday morning. Calmly, tactfully, Patrick explained the situation to her.

"I see. I'm sorry to hear that," she said with some sympathy. "I'll speak with Dr. Lauren right now; he's just come in. Please hold for just a moment." Patrick barely had time to say thank you before the receptionist was back on the line. "Dr. Lauren will be over in fifteen minutes, Mr. McKee," she told him.

"Oh. Thank you," Patrick said appreciatively. He exhaled loudly. "Thank you very much."

"Not a problem. Take care."

When he hung up the telephone, he closed his eyes, rubbed his whiskery chin, and took several deep breaths. He was stiff and sore from sleeping in that old rocking chair. His eyelids felt heavy as bricks.

There was a handsomely framed photograph of Rosemary on his desk, and his eyes were drawn to it now. She was a pretty woman, with soft, long-lashed brown eyes, plump, rosy cheeks and a sharp, dimpled chin. Never a flashy dresser, she preferred simple skirts and blouses, in various earth tones, and wore her fair wavy hair short, so that it curled up just above the collar. She had a habit of leaning—in doorways, against walls, furniture, lamp posts, trees, and so on—and hugging her chest below her bosom, a look of placid concentration on her face, as if she needed the support of something solid while she contemplated the world. In this particular photograph, taken at the family cottage, Rosemary leaned against an open sliding glass door but instead of hugging her chest she was cradling an orange-and-white striped cat—a stray who'd wandered onto the property. She was smiling, her eyes focused not on the camera lens but on something else just to the right of it and off a little in the distance.

Women were supposed to live longer than men, weren't they? Patrick had always heard that, though he'd never taken pause to seriously consider it before. He had simply believed he and Rosemary would live a long, happy life together—watch their children grow up, go to college, get married, have children of their own. And then, in their later years, slumped and greying and slower, maybe, but happy all the same, Patrick and Rosemary would take care of one another. They'd be grandparents—*proud* grandparents! And perhaps they'd do some travelling ....

He felt a shiver cross his shoulders and he looked away from the photograph, and wiped his eyes, which were moist with tears. Then he stood up straight, let out a long, tremulous breath, and told himself to buck up.

He headed down the hall to check on Maggie. She was just fine, sleeping peacefully in her darkened, purple room. And thankfully Finny was still asleep, too, though his little body twitched off and on, and his eyes fluttered as if he were dreaming something unpleasant. But at least he was sleeping. His father didn't dare wake him.

Patrick turned and proceeded downstairs to make some coffee and wait for the doctor to arrive. Dr. Lauren was a friend of Patrick's (they'd golfed together for years) and an excellent doctor, well-respected by his colleagues, thorough, seasoned, friendly. He'd helped deliver Maggie, in fact, back when he worked at Kingston Mercy Hospital as an obstetrician. It was a comfort knowing that Finny would be in good hands.

When Dr. Lauren knocked on the door, Patrick opened it for him holding a mug of warm coffee. A brisk breeze blew in, carrying the dank smell of an oncoming rain. Outside, it was a dreary morning. It must have rained recently. The street looked damp. Patrick quickly shut the door.

"Hi, David. Thank you for coming," Patrick said. "Especially on such short notice."

"Good to see you, Paddy," the doctor told him. "And it's not a problem at all; I hear we have a sick boy on our hands."

"We do, I'm afraid. Come in, come in."

Dr. Lauren wore a blue trench coat and carried a brown leather medical bag, his title and initials etched in gold italic lettering near the handle: *Dr. D.S. Lauren.* He smelled of some expensive cologne. He had neat black hair, and a handsome, trustworthy face. He also possessed a gentlemanly smile, Patrick thought—a phrase his mother liked to use. He looked quite a bit younger than a man in his fifties.

"Coffee?" Patrick offered.

The doctor shuffled his feet, wiping his sensible boots on the scruffy Welcome mat. "No, thank you. I've just had breakfast." The doctor smiled. "Finny's in his bedroom, is he?" he said.

Patrick shook his head no, but then he said, "Yes, he is. I'm sorry. I barely slept. You likely want to see him right away."

"Yes, I would," said the doctor.

"Of course. I'll show you upstairs," Patrick told him. "Don't worry about your boots." As they climbed the stairs, Patrick spoke over his shoulder. "Finny looks quite pale and he had quite a nightmare last night. Woke up hollering for his mother. He's not sleeping very much ... hasn't since, well—and he refuses to eat or drink anything. Or talk, for that matter. Also, he's been sucking his thumb, which I find sort of alarming."

"I see," said Dr. Lauren. They came to stand outside Finny's door. "And how is Maggie?"

"Maggie's fine," Patrick said. "She's very sad, of course, but she's coping well."

Dr. Lauren nodded his head. "Well, I'll have a look at Finny, give him a thorough check up, and see how he's doing. Shouldn't be more than half an hour."

"Thank you, David."

"You're quite welcome. He'll be just fine, I'm sure," said the doctor, and he clapped Patrick on the arm reassuringly.

While the doctor examined Finny, Patrick sat in his office and made several phone calls to work. Everything was fine, Nigel, the first floor manager, told him. Everything was under control and running smoothly; not to worry, he said. Patrick told him he'd be back to work in the next couple of days.

After the examination, Dr. Lauren and Patrick spoke at the kitchen table. This time, the doctor warmly accepted a mug of coffee. Patrick cupped his own mug with two hands, as if he might drop it if he used only one.

"Fortunately," said Dr. Lauren, "I can't find anything physically wrong with Finny. He's a strong, healthy boy, Paddy."

Finny's father nodded, relieved.

"Psychologically, however, he is clearly quite traumatized. He wonders why his mother had to die. He didn't say much but he was extremely attached to her, it seems."

"Yes, he was," said Patrick. "They were very close."

The doctor nodded. "Well," he said. "He's experienced a significant trauma at a very young age. It's not surprising he's so frightened."

"So he spoke?" said Finny's father, the thought just dawning on him.

"Yes, after a few minutes. Which is a good sign. He likely wasn't speaking to feel he had control over something. *Anything.*"

"I see."

"He needs to feel safe. Right now he thinks death is lurking around every corner. He needs to be reassured that it's *not,*" said Dr. Lauren, strongly emphasizing the last word.

"Okay."

"His world's been turned upside down, essentially. What he needs now is to feel loved and safe. He needs human interaction, a sense of normalcy. He mentioned a friend of his—Fiona; he said he'd like to see her."

"He did?"

"Yes. And I think it's an excellent idea if he does. Spending some time with someone his own age will be helpful. And he would certainly benefit from being outdoors—the fresh air will do him a world of good. It's unhealthy for him to be locked away in his room."

"Of course."

"And I would also strongly suggest that you hire a nanny."

"A *nanny?*" said Finny's father.

"Someone to read to the boy, distract him, take his mind off things. Wear him out before bedtime. I know you're a busy man, Paddy. This must be taking its toll on you as well."

Patrick sighed heavily. "Maybe so," he said, immersed in thought.

"You have the resources," Dr. Lauren pointed out.

"Right," said Finny's father.

"Find someone who's experienced and good with children, preferably someone who has children of their own."

The doctor stood up and gave Patrick's arm a firm squeeze. He'd barely touched his coffee. "Gradual steps," he said. "Think of it that way. Take one thing at a time. Finny will come around soon enough, I'm sure of it. So will you, and so will Maggie."

"Well, thank you," said Patrick. He stood up and the two men shook hands.

"I'm truly sorry for your loss," the doctor said kindly. "Grieving takes time. Remember that. Allow yourself time to grieve. Finny and Maggie need time to grieve, too."

There was a brief silence. Then the doctor said, "Meantime, I'll leave you with this." And he handed Finny's father a crisp blue business card. "That's Dr. Oliver's information. She's an excellent young therapist who works with children. If you feel Finny's not improving—not sleeping, having nightmares, and such, or even if you feel he needs just to talk to someone—give her a call. And Maggie might benefit from speaking with her as well."

Patrick nodded at the card, squinting his eyes to read the small print.

"And as for *right now*," Dr. Lauren added in a chummy tone, "I recommend you make the boy some toast and scrambled eggs. He didn't say as much, but he's likely starving."

Patrick allowed himself to smile, then, if only slightly. He was relieved to hear that his son was talking, and would, it seemed, recover well in due time. Still, his mind remained cluttered with troubling thoughts, and his insides felt hollowed out yet heavy with the deadweight of loss.

He saw the doctor out and stood at the door for a time, watching some leaves blow around in the gutter.

Years later, in *The Orphan Diaries*, Finny's largely autobiographical first novel, Finny would write: "After my mother died, my father became tense, distracted, and withdrew into long, impenetrable silences. His world, it was clear, was all but shattered. The unthinkable death of my mother, only thirty-two at the time, truly broke his heart."

<div align="center">~~~~~</div>

Still ... never one to waste time, Patrick hired a nanny two days later. The woman—highly recommended by a business associate of Patrick's who ran a first-rate daycare centre—had plenty of experience and glowing references. When Finny's father introduced his children to their new nanny in the rarely-used, cavernous living room, he said: "Maggie, Finny, this is Ana—Ana with one *n*."

Then he explained that Ana would be staying with them six nights a week—every night but Sunday. She would cook, clean, do laundry, and watch over them when he wasn't home.

"She's tiny," Maggie whispered in Finny's ear.

This was true. For an adult, Ana was short. (*Little* was the word that first came to Finny's mind.) If she was five feet tall, it was because of the thick heels on her white tennis shoes.

She smiled at them shyly, prettily. She was quite pretty, Finny thought, with a bob of shiny black hair, a button nose, and bright brown eyes accentuated by very long eyelashes.

"It's very nice to meet you," Ana said. She had a Portuguese accent, just like Jesse, the janitor at Finny's school. (When Finny stayed after school to play floor hockey in the gymnasium with his buddies, Jesse would remind them to "close the lights" when they were done.)

Maggie held out her hand clumsily, but said in a cheerful voice, "It's nice to meet you, too. I'm Maggie."

Ana shook her hand, smiled sunnily and nodded, as if making some mental note. "Maggie," she said. "A very pretty name."

Maggie blushed. "Thank you," she said. "You have a pretty name too."

Ana turned to Finny, whose first reaction was to step back a foot and press up against his sister. Ana noted his apprehension. Gently, softly, she said, "And you must be Finny," and her eyes met his only briefly, as not to make him any more uncomfortable than he already was.

Normally, Finny was frightened by strangers. But, despite his initial, instinctive reaction, he was not frightened by Ana.

Soon enough, he and Maggie would learn that Ana was born in Portugal but had lived in Canada since she was a little girl—Finny's age, in fact. She had two children of her own, was divorced, and lived in a small north end apartment above a camera store with not only her two children (two girls) to look after but her mother, as well. Apparently her mother had suffered some sort of mental breakdown some years before, needed a great deal of care, and could not live on her own. Fortunately, Ana had a sister, Bianca, who lived not a block away and could be counted on to look after Ana's girls and their mother when Ana was working. They also discovered that Ana's husband was a "deadbeat dad," who now lived in Winnipeg and contributed nothing financially to help out Ana or her daughters. It was from Ana that they learned all this—she was sweet, forthright and extremely chatty. Finny and Maggie took to her almost instantly; it was difficult not to, she exuded such a simple, acquiescent charm. She was warmhearted and naturally engaging. They followed her around the house as she dusted mantels, scrubbed the bath tub, folded laundry, and polished furniture. Ana talked and talked as she worked, and the children peppered her with question after question.

Ana was also a lot of fun. "Magically," she produced quarters from behind Finny's ears and did a trick with her hands that made it look like she'd pulled off the end of her thumb, which sent Maggie into silly giggling fits. When she put away Finny's laundry, she would playfully hold a pair of Finny's socks to her nose and crinkle up her face at him, which he thought was singularly hilarious. "What an awful, horrible smell," she'd say, clucking her tongue. "I think we need stronger washing detergent." Sprawled across his bed, Finny laughed and laughed. His cheeks turned red, and he hid his head beneath his pillow in mock shame.

At night, Ana gathered the children in Maggie's room. She tucked Maggie and Finny snugly under the purple blankets and comforters on Maggie's frilly, canopy bed and read to them from a thick, hard-covered book called *Treasured Childhood Stories*. In a silky, animated voice, Ana read to them about fascinating creatures who lived in enchanting, faraway lands, handsome princes and beautiful princesses, pirates and buried treasure. Maggie was typically quick to fall asleep, but Finny was not. An afternoon of walks and bike rides and playing badminton and Frisbee in the backyard failed to tire him out. Thankfully, Ana possessed endless energy and a great deal of patience. Once Maggie was asleep, Ana took Finny to his own room, tucked him under his own covers, and read to him from the dictionary, as his mother had. Her method was like Finny's mother's as well; she opened the dictionary and read words at random. Finny liked the sound of Ana's voice. Her accent was charming. It made the hairs on the back of his neck stand up. He could have listened to her all night, but eventually, thankfully—for both of them—after Ana had read for fifteen or twenty minutes, Finny would fall over the edge into sleep.

But then, again and again, he would wake up screaming, calling out for his mother, certain his rapidly beating heart would explode.

Ana was always quick to respond. She wore a sort of nurse's uniform, as Finny thought of it, even in the middle of the night—a white skirt and blouse, white tennis shoes and a knitted blue cardigan. Finny imagined she sat alertly in a chair in the hallway all night, like a security guard, even though she'd be given one of the guest rooms as her own. He could not recall ever seeing her yawn.

"Hush now," Ana soothed him. "You'll wake the neighbourhood." She smiled and massaged Finny's shoulders. "You'll wake the whole city. Jeepers creepers."

As a rule, Finny disliked being touched, but, again, he felt differently with Ana. Her hands were small and soft, and she seemed to know precisely where to rub his back and shoulders to relax his tensed up little body. Sometimes she made gentle little circles on Finny's temples with her fingertips, and he would grow calm, his breathing would slow, and he would all but collapse into sleep.

One night in November, he told her he was beginning to forget what his mother looked like. A mean hail battered his bedroom window. Thunder clapped and shook the house every thirty seconds or so.

"When you close your eyes," Ana said, "and think of your mother, what do you see?"

Finny shut his eyes. "A lady in a summer hat watching the waves on the water."

"That's wonderful," Ana said, sounding genuinely pleased. "Now—is she smiling? Do her eyes look happy?" she asked him.

"I can't tell. I can't see her face."

"Oh, dear heart, sure you can. Try harder."

"But I can't see her face."

"What colour are her eyes, Finny?" Ana asked him.

"Brown," he said.

"Light brown or dark brown?"

"Light brown."

"And is there a smile on her face?"

"Yes," Finny said. He began to cry. Quietly.

"She's very pretty, no?"

"She's beautiful," Finny said.

"Like an angel," Ana added.

"Like an angel," Finny said.

"Now, hold that picture in your mind," Ana told him, "and never let it go. If you keep that picture in your mind, your mother will be with you, always, no matter where you are. Okay?"

"Okay," Finny said, and tears spilled down his cheeks as he began to cry harder. Ana pulled him gently into a hug and made circles on his back with both hands.

"I could not explain it or express it then, and perhaps I cannot properly do either now," Finny wrote, more than a decade later, in *The Orphan Diaries*, "but in those moments I felt a very real sense of peace, of release and relief. And if I could replicate those feelings at will, I would summon them often. But sadly I cannot."

~~~~~~

Fiona began coming over again for visits. She lived four houses away in an imposingly large, limestone house with wrought iron gates at the entrance to the driveway and a four-foot limestone wall surrounding the entire property. It was a convenient one-minute walk from Fiona's front door to Finny's front door, and so, once Finny began eating and speaking again, Fiona came by often.

On a Saturday afternoon, they stretched out side by side on Finny's bed, Fiona pointing her View-Master at the light of the ceiling fan, Finny with his Etch-A-Sketch balanced across his knees.

"Which one are you looking at?" Finny asked.
~~~~~~

"Jasper National Park," Fiona said. "Wanna see?"

"Nah."

Finny had trouble with curves. He was trying to draw a unicycle but couldn't get it right. "Geez," he said, and then, "Dammit." Fiona yawned and looked through her View-Master, going *click ... click ... click*. She switched positions, resting her head on Finny's stomach, her stockinged feet up on the wall. Finny groaned and gave his Etch-A-Sketch a good hearty shake, erasing what he'd drawn. Then Fiona put her View-Master down and said, "I wish my mother had died instead."

Her mother was a bully, and Finny disliked her. An angry, jittery, short-tempered woman, Mrs. Walters frightened him. (Fiona never said much about her father, though Finny knew he was a quiet man, distant, remote; he stayed out of things.) When Finny and Fiona spent time together, therefore, they mostly spent it at Finny's house.

"But my mother would go to hell," Fiona said. "Your mother is in heaven. Don't you think?"

"I guess," Finny said quietly. He felt strange. Confused. He wanted to talk about his mother and then he didn't. He wished he was invisible. He wished he and Fiona could run away together and live in a tree fort or a motel.

They grew bored, put on their shoes, and Finny told Ana that he and Fiona were going to play in the backyard. Instead, they wandered down to the boat house. They had a favourite spot—a sort of loft high above where the tethered boat rocked slightly in the water. They had to climb a ladder to get up there, where tools hung on the cedar walls and a big, round window let in the afternoon sunshine. To sit on, they took a wool blanket and spread it across an inflatable bedlike raft. They shared a bottle of Coke, hung their legs over the side of the walkway, and listened to the water splashing against the boat house door. Sunlight warmed their backs.

"What do you want for your birthday?" Fiona asked. As usual, she was the one to begin the conversation.

"What?" Finny sent her a puzzled look. "My birthday's in *July*."

"So? Geez—just play along. Pretend your birthday's tomorrow. What would you wish for?"

"Dunno," Finny told her.

"Oh, come on! Name one thing, one little thing in the whole wide world. A record player. A new bike. A guitar. A trip to Disneyland. You must want something."

Finny said, "A one iron."

"A what?"

"A golf club; a one iron."

"Oh," Fiona said, sounding disappointed. She wasn't athletic in the least; she was musically inclined. She played piano, and she was excellent. Played at school assemblies. Won competitions. Took lessons—sometimes three a day—from a first-rate teacher, a graduate of the Juilliard School in New York who now taught in the music department at Queen's University. Fiona said, "Well, that's nice, I guess."

"I bet I could hit one two-hundred yards, straight as an arrow," Finny told her. "I've done it on the range, but it'd be much cooler on the course where you actually have something to aim at."

"The flag thingie," said Fiona.

Finny sighed. "The flag *stick*. The pin. How many times do I have to tell you? Geez."

"Well, I don't know. I was close."

Finny groaned.

They grew bored again. Finny told Ana as much, and that they were taking a city bus downtown to visit his father at the department store. Folding laundry, she said okay, that would be fine.

McKee & Sons was a huge, four-storey, L-shaped limestone building on the corner of Main and Front Streets. When they got there, Finny and Fiona took the elevator straight up to the fourth floor, which was one long, colossal storage room filled with shoes and clothing, house wares and fine china, boxes of candy and sports equipment. Fiona immediately grabbed a woman's wig and put it in on the body of a naked male mannequin.

"Very nice," Finny told her. He snared a pitching wedge and a handful of plastic golf balls from a dusty golf display case, then began chipping the balls off a navy blue, plush bath mat. A mini-trampoline about fifteen yards away was his target—he thought of it as a small, blue green. The ceiling was high, and the white plastic balls arced through the musty air, bouncing high off the mini-trampoline almost every time (Finny was an outstanding wedge player) and landing near an unplugged Pepsi machine. The balls rolled around the cold cement floor and came to rest in a sunken spot, near an open cardboard box overflowing with snorkels and yellow masks and water wings.

"Check it out," Fiona said, gesturing toward the male mannequin she'd dressed in a pink baby doll dress and multicoloureded French beret. "He is ver-eee chic, *non?*" she said in a horrible French accent.

"*Non,*" Finny said, but he had to laugh.

Later they sat in matching maroon wing chairs by one of the floor-to-ceiling windows overlooking Main Street. Finny gobbled down a large bag of dill pickle chips, while Fiona, wearing a deerstalker hat and a man's safari jacket, crossed her legs and pretended to smoke a pipe.

"Whatever shall we have for dinner, *daw-ling?*" she asked, trying to sound grown up, sophisticated, haughty.

Finny played along. "Fries and gravy, I should think," he said, in a similar tone, and Fiona fell into a giggling fit. "With Pogos on the side," he added. "And bottomless jugs of ice cold Dr Pepper."

Fiona laughed so hard she nearly fell out of her wing chair.

A saleslady entered the room. She was looking for something, but stopped short and clutched her chest when she saw Finny and Fiona. She was an older lady, forty-something, wearing too much makeup, a white blouse and pleated black slacks. Her hair was black, too, and perfectly feathered.

"Oh my," she said, hand over her heart. "You scared me silly."

By her tone, Finny could tell she recognized him—and maybe Fiona, too.

"Sorry," Finny told her.

"Oh, that's okay," she said sweetly. She sighed, then seemed to remember what she'd come for; she began rifling through a rack of women's skirts. "All these smalls and mediums and larges," she said, mainly to herself. "Who in the world takes an extra small?"

Finny thought of Ana. *She* might wear extra small clothing, he thought.

"I'm hungry," Finny said, after the saleslady had gone. "Wanna get something to eat?"

"But you just ate a whole huge bag of chips."

Finny shrugged.

"Okay, I guess."

So they took the elevator down to the first floor, where there was a lunch counter between the men's clothing and sporting goods' departments, and sat down beside one another on red swiveling stools.

"Hey, kids," said Ruth, a rake-thin woman with long red hair pulled back into a pony tail high on her head, extremely pale skin, and a face full of freckles. "What'll it be?"

She smiled at Finny and tousled his curly hair.

"Hi, Ruth," he said.

"Hey, kiddo," Ruth said.

"Hiya, Ruthie," Fiona said brightly.

Ruth's smile widened and she winked at Fiona, whom she absolutely adored. Sometimes she would let Fiona come around the counter and help one of the line cooks flip pancakes or scramble eggs or stir a huge pot of homemade chili. Fiona, meantime, peppered Ruth with endless questions about her husband and her family. "Why would anyone want to join the army?" she'd ask Ruth, whose husband was a radar operator at CFB Kingston. To that, Ruth would shrug and ask Fiona why she wore army fatigues and boots if she disliked the army so much.

"I don't like the army because they *kill* people," she'd explained to Ruth, more than once. "I like their clothes, though. They're comfortable."

Fiona tended to wear baggy clothes: men's large sweaters, plaid flannel shirts three times too big for her, ripped army pants with saggy rear ends. Her dark black hair was cut short, curled around her ears, and occasionally her bangs were uneven as she often cut them herself and, well, sometimes it showed. Still, she was very pretty, and Ruth often told her as much. It was her eyes, Ruth said. Those big, mischievous, velvety brown eyes.

"I'll have a chocolate shake, please," Fiona told Ruth. "And Finnyboy wants fries and gravy even though he just wolfed down a whole huge bag of chips."

"Don't call me that," Finny said.

"Okay, *Finnegan*," Fiona teased.

Finny made an ugly face. "Or that," he said. "Especially that."

Finnegan was his real name. He hated it. Thankfully, aside from Fiona when she wanted to bug him, no one ever called him that.

After they'd finished (Fiona had changed her mind and ordered a slice of apple pie), Ruth leaned on the counter and begged Fiona to play a song on the big display piano which, for some reason, was in the sporting goods' section.

Fiona's cheeks grew rosy. For all her talent, she was shy about playing in public. "Oh, I don't know," she said.

"Oh, please please please, sugar pie," Ruth pleaded, batting her eyelashes. "Won't you just play one itty-bitty song?"

"Oh, all right, already."

"Yay!" Ruth caroled.

"Good stuff," said Bernie, the big, bashful line cook on duty.

Fiona sat herself down at the piano, her posture perfect. She cracked her knuckles, which made Finny wince. He sat on a chair a few feet away, flanked by racks of sneakers and soccer cleats, resting his chin on his fists.

Fiona played a song she always played for Ruth, a song Finny recognized but couldn't name right away. Then it came to him: "Your Song" by Elton John. Fiona played wonderfully and you could see her mouthing the words to herself, silently. A few shoppers stopped and listened, smiles on their faces. Dan, the salesman from sporting goods who had recently been expelled from high school for selling marijuana, listened too, a glazed yet enchanted look in his eyes. Meantime, Ruth sang along quietly:

> *I hope you don't mind*
> *I hope you don't mind*
> *That I put down in words*
> *How wonderful life is while you're in the world*

Fiona cut the song short, and Ruth and Bernie clapped enthusiastically. Dan applauded as well, and added a loud, friendly whistle. Fiona put her hands over her eyes and giggled. She peeked through her fingers and made funny eyes at Finny, who had been smiling the whole time.

~~~~~~

Despite his many fears and bashful nature, Finny breezed through elementary school. He was a fine student, well liked by his teachers. His marks were excellent, he excelled at sports and had a small circle of loyal friends. Generally, Finny was happy, although he was still quite fearful. Also, he felt like a fraud.

His biggest fear was reading in front of his classmates. The mere thought of having to do so made him queasy, quite literally, and aroused a whirlwind of skittish, panicky thoughts in his mind. Therefore, he had to be crafty.

He acted the class clown. It seemed to Finny the best trick of all. If you were jokey and witty and charming enough, Finny discovered, it was like you were disguised. In the teacher's eyes, you came across as assertive, gregarious, sharp, playful. You hammed it up. You were a gas and got your classmates to laughing. (It was actually sort of rush for Finny, being able to crack everyone up so easily, teachers included.) You were silly, maybe, but clever and confident. You were, as most of Finny's teachers noted in his report cards, "a pleasure to have in class." Finny had no difficulty answering questions in class, mainly because he knew the right answers, then add a twist of humour and—*presto!*—you were not only bright but charming; a star, a
~~~~~~

golden boy, a near model student. And so it was like you'd filled your quota, so to speak, and teachers didn't feel the need to bother you more by asking you to read a passage from a text.

Finny had other tricks as well—back ups, really, in case the class rogue facade didn't work. They were simple enough. One trick Finny thought of as *dodging*. For instance: when everyone in class was sitting in a circle, each reading a section of a book, Finny would simply ask to use the washroom. But his timing had to be perfect. If he asked too soon, there was a chance he'd come back and still have to read. Alternately, if he asked too late—say, when the kid beside him was about to read—a teacher might say, "Can't you wait until it's your turn?" That had happened a few times, but Finny had been quick on his toes. "I really can't," he'd said, jostling about and looking uncomfortable, and of course he'd been excused. Then he'd stayed in the washroom for a long time, until just before recess or lunch or the end of the school day, so there was no danger that when he returned to class a teacher would remember he'd missed his turn and go back to him to read. It wouldn't have mattered; time was up.

And if that failed, another simple trick was claiming a sore throat. It was obvious, sure, so you couldn't use it too much. In eight years at Highgate Park Elementary, Finny'd only used the sore throat bit a handful of times, but it had worked without fail.

"I still find it odd," Finny wrote, "that none of my teachers caught on and recognized just how fearful I was, but it seems I managed to maneuver just below their radar, day after day, year after year, playing the role of witty class clown."

Until grade eight, that was, with Ms. Plumb. She was a shrewd, stern disciplinarian—an uptight spinsterly woman who wore drab polyester dresses and clompy brown shoes—so it shouldn't have surprised Finny that she would finally be the one to find him out. But it did. On his report card, dated 19 December 1981, Ms. Plumb wrote: "Finny is genuinely well liked by his classmates and generally a pleasure to have in class. He is a very diligent, highly intelligent young man. However," she noted, "he often ducks out of reading in class, and when called upon to answer a question, he repeatedly acts out to get attention."

It was true. Finny couldn't deny it. She was bang on. Even the wording, *Ducks out of reading* ....

His heart sunk. He had to sit down on the curb where he waited for his bus. "Read this," he told Fiona, passing her the report. He thought he might be sick.

"What?" She began reading.

"I'm doomed," Finny said. "Shit. She'll stand me at the blackboard and make me read entire textbooks from January to June."

"Oh boy," Fiona said finally.

"And my dad has to sign the thing, too," Finny said. "Oh my God. I think I'm gonna puke."

He bent over, hanging his head between his knees like someone on a plane preparing for a crash landing.

"Well, don't have a conniption," Fiona said. "Really, it's not that bad. I mean, what can she do about it? Besides, you have straight A's. Your dad can't complain about that. So you're not the world's best public speaker. Big whoop! Check out what she wrote on mine. 'Has forgotten or misplaced her gym clothes on seventeen occasions since September.' *Seventeen*—like she's been meticulously recording this shit. Like she has nothing better to do with her life, the crabby old spinster! She called me a 'daydreaming silly heart.'"

"My dad will send me to the Dale Carnegie Institute," Finny said forlornly.

"He will not."

"He will. He'll say, 'How do you expect to ever make something of yourself acting this way?' I know he will. He wants me to help him run his store someday. Take over when he retires. He'll freak when he reads this. 'How will you ever run the family business behaving like a coward?' he'll say."

"But you don't even want to work for your father," Fiona said.

"I won't," Finny said. "I never will."

"So what does it matter, then? You're making too much of this, Finny. Or I know!" she said excitedly. "I'll *forge* his signature. He'll never have to know a thing!"

Finny groaned. "Fee, don't be stupid. My father knows we get report cards before Christmas. He'll *want* to see it."

Fiona made a face, looking wounded. She crinkled up her nose. "Well, fine, then," she said sulkily. "There's no need to be mean about it."

They were quiet a moment.

Then Finny said, "I'm sorry."

"It's okay," Fiona told him.

In the end, it turned out, Fiona was right: Finny was making too much of it; at least when it came to his father. An outgoing, sociable, assertive type by nature, Patrick was troubled by Ms. Plumb's comments, of course, but he didn't flip out like Finny imagined he would. He sat at his desk, tie loosened, tipped back casually in his black leather chair, and read over the report. Finny sat stiffly in a similar chair across from him.

"All A's," Finny pointed out.

"I can see that. That's excellent, Finny. But this here," he said.

"She has a steel plate in her head," Finny told his father, so quickly he all but startled himself. "I think she has me mixed up with someone else."

Patrick let out a little laugh. "Whatsay?"

"Seriously. She was hit by a truck or something when she was a little girl and had to have a steel plate put in her head. Everyone knows about it." Finny gulped. "She gets confused sometimes. Sometimes she forgets our names."

"Hmm," said Patrick. He lowered his eyebrows and combed his hair to the left with his fingers, something he did when he was getting tired. He yawned.

Finny smiled innocently and shrugged his shoulders. "She must have made a mistake."

"A mistake?"

"I guess. She's a little bonkers, Dad. I mean, it's not her fault but—"

"*Do you* duck out of reading in class?"

"No," Finny said. "Never." He was amazed at how easily the lies escaped his lips.

"Do you act out when asked a question?"

"No!" Finny said pointedly, adding a confused laugh for emphasis.

"Well," said Patrick. He looked at the report card again. Then, "All right," he said, and scribbled his signature on it.

Finny was relieved beyond words.

But the real trouble came the first week in January, when Ms. Plumb assigned the class a book report. Finny was sure she'd hatched the idea just to pick on him. At any rate, he was petrified by the thought of standing in front of his classmates and reading, so one day when everyone else was heading outside for recess, Finny stayed behind and then sat down in a chair next to Ms. Plumb, who was sitting at her desk making tiny notes in a blue ledger book. Nervously, Finny asked her if he could write *two* book reports on separate books instead of reading *one* report to the class.

Ms. Plumb looked at him with narrowed eyes. She was silent a few moments. The frown lines around her mouth deepened. Her cardigan stank of stale cigarette smoke.

"But the point of reading the report to the class," she said, "is to help build your public speaking skills, Finny. To make you a more confident speaker."

"I know," Finny said. "But writing two reports will help build my *writing* skills."

She studied his face carefully, as if she thought she could gauge something important in his expression. Finny tried to look at ease, anything but how he felt: agitated, distraught, desperate.

"Well," said Ms. Plumb. "That much is true."

"It would also help build my comprehension skills," Finny added. He hoped he didn't sound like he was pleading. Although that's very much what it felt like to Finny: like he was a prisoner pleading not to be tortured. He held his hands together between his legs so they would not shake.

"I suppose," said Ms. Plumb. "But your comprehension skills are already superior, Finny. And I'm not normally one to make exceptions. It's a dangerous practice."

Finny nodded, though he couldn't imagine how making an exception in this case might be dangerous. But wait—she'd said *normally*. There was hope! Finny all but held his breath as Ms. Plumb furrowed her eyebrows, deliberating, for what seemed like an eternity.

"All right," she said finally. "You can write two reports."

An intoxicating feeling of relief surged through Finny's system. He inhaled deeply, then released a long, grateful sigh.

"Thank you," he said.

"But no more funny business in class," Ms. Plumb told him sternly. "No more sarcastic remarks, no more horse play, and no more jokes at my expense."

"No more," Finny said, respectfully. "None. Ever again."

He couldn't have been more sincere.

Immensely grateful and relieved, Finny dutifully kept his promise. For the rest of the year, he was truly a model student. He did not act out. He stifled his sarcasm, saved the jokes for recess, and when he answered questions, he did so politely, humbly, with a reflective sort of sincerity. He'd learned his lesson; he wasn't about to blow his second chance.

In lieu of horse play, as Ms. Plumb had called it, Finny took to writing in his journal. Well, more accurately, to *printing* in his journal—his handwriting was atrocious. He enjoyed observing people—after all, he'd done so quietly, bashfully, for years—and he also liked writing down his thoughts. Happily, he noted, in printing so neat and small it resembled typewriting, that Mario Delitti had a crush on Fiona and Fiona was flattered but claimed she could never go out with a boy who always smelled like salami. (Mario's father was a butcher.) Finny carefully considered his classmates: Sarah Billsworth wore pink far too often, in Finny's opinion, especially for someone so fair-skinned, and Joey Strouse, though popular and handsome and a good athlete, was a kleptomaniac and likely, Finny mused, headed for prison some day. And when exactly had Margaret Miller developed such large breasts? She was half a foot taller than any other girl in the class, too, which also seemed a recent development. Class was in a shabby, yellow portable set about a fifty meters away from the school. The lights flickered, the walls creaked, and the heating system was loud and unreliable. Finny dutifully, gratifyingly jotted all this down, as Ms. Plumb sat on the edge of her desk and read *Of Mice And Men* to the class. Beside him, Fiona tilted a drawing his way—a piano with wings. Finny smiled and gave her a thumbs up. She smiled happily herself, pleased with her artwork.

After school, they walked downtown to McKee's and goofed around in the storage room or shared a plate of fries and gravy at the first-floor diner. They studied together in their favourite spot in the boat house, smoking French cigarettes Fiona had pinched from her mother's purse. If her mother ever caught her stealing cigarettes, Fiona was in for a beating, but she told Finny, "Screw it. Maybe that'd be a good thing. Maybe one of these days she'll take things too far and a neighbour will see her bashing me with a rolling pin and the cops will come and take her away."

"Why don't *you* just call the cops?" Finny asked her.

Fiona shook her head, not answering the question. "She thinks I owe her the world," she said, "just because I spent nine months in her womb. Like I owe her for just existing. I wish my father had never married her."

"But then you'd never have been born."

"Exactly."

In May, Finny was selected class valedictorian. During recess one day, while Ms. Plumb walked the school grounds with a string of younger kids seemingly attached to her cardigan, Finny thanked her for choosing him. He was truly flattered, he said, but wondered if Fiona might not be a better choice. Her marks were just as good as his, and she was a better speaker, besides—more animated. And people took her seriously. Finny was more of the stand up comic type, he thought.

Ms. Plumb seemed unsurprised at Finny's reluctance. It was like she was challenging him, Finny thought. Actually, he was sure that's what she was doing. She told the children to run along, which they did, then when they were standing alone, she said to Finny, "You know, you can't avoid the things you fear your whole life, Finny. At some point, you have to face them, and the sooner you do, the sooner you'll overcome them."

Her tone was kind. Finny looked at a spot just over her shoulder.

"I'm just not built that way," he said.

"High school won't be any easier, you know. You can't simply walk between the rain drops. No matter who you are."

That reminded Finny of something his father would say.

He felt torn. On the one hand, he liked being honoured as valedictorian; he also loved writing and felt he had a lot to say, some of it funny, some of it serious and significant. On the other, he couldn't imagine how he could pull off giving a speech to a hundred or so people, including his father. Then it came to him, a grand idea: he could write a speech and then read it into a tape recorder. He pictured it: on the gymnasium stage he would sit the tape recorder on a wooden stool next to a microphone and press Play, then step aside and let his words ring out. There was no need for people to actually *see* him read the speech; it was hearing the words that mattered, wasn't it?

He was overcome by a sudden jolt of excitement.

"Forget what I said," he told Ms. Plumb. "I'll do it."

This time, she looked surprised. "Well, good," she said. "I'm glad."

Finny wondered if she would be glad in the end. But he didn't say so. He thanked her again and went to look for Fiona.

Over the next few weeks, he worked diligently on the speech. Fiona came by his house after piano lessons to read it over and offer her opinion. Finny didn't want the thing to be cliché; he wanted it to be real. And so much of it was about fear, and what Finny thought was fair and unfair, a point which he hoped to drill home by using his tape recorder. Fiona thought it was ingenious.

And it worked out pretty much how Finny had pictured it. When he was introduced, he strode up to the podium very much at ease, although his heart was beating fast as the audience applauded heartily. He wore a handsome cream-coloured suit with a red tie and brown dress shoes. As he stood at the podium, he felt a rush of fear and exhilaration. The applause petered out. He set the tape recorder on the podium, plucked the microphone off its stand and placed it next to the recorder, smiled, and pressed down on the Play button. Then he backed up a few feet and stood there, blank-faced, hands stuffed in his trouser pockets, as his voice began to echo throughout the high-ceilinged gymnasium: "Good evening ladies and gentlemen, my fellow graduates, faculty. I would like to ask this of each and every one of you: What is your greatest fear?"

Finny was afraid the sound might come across as tinny, but it did not. His voice was clear. He avoided looking at his father, Maggie, Ana, and Fiona's parents.

There was a general murmur among the crowd. People looked sideways at one another. A few students laughed. A lady (someone's aunt or mother) said, "What on earth?"

The recording continued: "Have you ever thought about it? Have you ever faced it? Has it ever kept you up at night and made you wonder if you could go on?"

In the end, most in attendance agreed, the address itself was remarkably candid, even parts clever and poignant and comical, and suitably forward-looking. Most also agreed the presentation was remarkably odd, which Finny accepted as complimentary. When the speech was over and the tape recorder fell silent, the audience applauded generously, students whistled, and Principal Simmons looked genuinely confused but clapped his hands, all the same. Meanwhile, Finny picked up his tape recorder and bowed graciously, one single nod of his head. While his stomach did flip-flops and his heart thudded away in his chest, he ate up the applause and felt charged by an overpowering, lightheaded, electrical surge of feelings that he could only guess came as a result of sheer euphoria.

~~~~~~

The trick to doing well in high school, Finny quickly discovered, was doing what was expected of you. You could get away with less, but that was risky. You could draw more attention to yourself that way, and that wasn't at all what Finny wanted. No, best to appear confident, attentive, busy, and do what you were asked. Finny nodded a lot, smiled at appropriate times, and took copious amounts of notes.

Finny's high school—Breckenridge Secondary—was enormous and dizzyingly crowded: fifteen hundred students crammed into a sprawling, squat brown-brick building that, from the outside, resembled a factory. Inside, miles of corridors led you to one staircase or another—or to a gymnasium or a courtyard or an exit. The cafeteria, to Finny's golfer's eye, must have been a hundred and fifty yards long, a bank of tall windows on the back wall offering a view of a parking lot and the football field. There were countless rows of foldable tables and chairs, a fleet of vending machines, and a separate room where hot food was served. It took Finny a week to locate the library, which was actually just above the cafeteria, across from the music rooms which were filled with an impressive selection of instruments: cellos, violins, tubas, saxophones, keyboards, acoustic guitars, drums, and so on. It was easy enough to get lost in such a bustling, bewilderingly huge place. It was just as easy to *feel* lost, as well.

For the first month or so, Finny frequently felt lost. Muddled. Overwhelmed. There were so many new faces to
~~~~~~

look at in the flooded hallways and things to learn and remember—rules, names, schedules, locker combinations—it was exhausting. On top of all this came school work, and lots of it.

Finny and Fiona saw little of each other during the day. She was enrolled in an enriched music program, so their schedules were misaligned, although they did get to spend forty-five minutes together for lunch. They both disliked the cafeteria—it was loud and congested and the hot food tasted like cardboard—so they went off school grounds and ate at a funky little diner across the street called The Malt Shop. They ordered cheeseburgers, Pogos, onion rings or fries topped with rich beef gravy, and sometimes Fiona had a slice of homemade pie while Finny gulped down a chocolate milkshake. The owner was a woman named Felicia who dressed like a gypsy, played Joni Mitchell songs all day and sang and twirled behind the counter, as she blended milkshakes and whipped up decadent banana splits blanketed with hot fudge. Finny thought she was sweet in an eccentric sort of way, but Fiona loved her to bits and they got along like chummy sisters.

"Where did you get that hat?" Fiona would ask her, for Felicia was always wearing some sort of exotic hat: a velvet derby, a wool mod cap, a maroon beret, and today a straw-cloth hat with an upturned brim and an artificial red rose adorning one side.

"Oh, this one—well, I can't really say for sure," said Felicia, humming and bobbing and drumming her fingers on a coffee pot as Joni Mitchell sang "Big Yellow Taxi." "I find them here and there, you know. At flea markets, thrift stores, antique shops, and big old garage sales. I've a whole walk-in closet filled entirely with hats. My mother always wore a hat and she always looked so elegant, so distinctive. I guess that's why I like them."

Finny pictured his mother, who often wore a wide-brimmed straw hat while painting. Or, at least, he tried to picture her; he could never keep an image of her in his mind's eye very long. He was beginning to forget what she looked and sounded like, the way she moved, how she smelled. It saddened him a great deal that even his memory of her was gradually slipping away.

"*You* should wear a hat!" Felicia told Fiona. The way she said it, it sounded like an order.

Fiona looked startled. "I should?"

"Sure. You have the most perfectly regal cheek bones and pretty brown eyes. Something dark, something brown—a wool felt bowler! You'd look like a movie star. All the boys would be after you."

"Fat chance," Fiona sniffled.

"Don't you dare say that."

"Boys don't like me," Fiona said. "I intimidate them."

Felicia looked at Finny.

He smiled. "We're just friends," he told her.

"Best friends since grade one," Fiona added. "I've never had a real boyfriend."

"Oh. Well. That's a shame."

"Not really. I'll get one when I want one," Fiona told her, and Felicia laughed.

"That's the attitude," she said. "You just take your time and wait for the right one to come along. A boy with moxie. A boy who'll put you up on a pedestal and treat you like a queen. A boy with something more than bedroom eyes."

Fiona giggled.

"So I guess you're not married?" Finny said.

Felicia looked at him slyly. "Ha!" she said. "You're a fresh one. I like that in a man."

Finny felt embarrassed but he allowed himself to smile.

"Best friends or not," Felicia whispered to Fiona, with a wink, "you keep a close eye on this one."

Fiona's face turned as red as the rose on the side of Felicia's hat.

After they'd eaten, they stood outside a nearby pet store and shared a long menthol cigarette. (Fiona's mother had changed brands.) They watched a litter of beagle puppies playing in the front window. The tiny dogs friskily bumped heads and loafed around in shredded newspaper.

"Oh, my. Don't you just want to set them all free?" Fiona said.

"I'm sure they'll all get bought up," Finny said.

"They're just so cute and clumsy," Fiona said. "I could just scoop them up and take them all home with me. Or, well, take them somewhere, anyway."

Fiona hated her mother, who had been increasingly abusive in recent months, and thus Fiona hated her home. The day she turned eighteen, Fiona had vowed countless times, she was gone, out the door with her red vintage suitcase, without one single look back, even if she had to live at the YWCA and work two jobs to support herself. That would be a thousand times better than living with her mother's furious slaps and wicked tirades.

If Finny had his way, he'd have Mrs. Walters taken away by the cops and locked up. But it was slightly more complicated than that because Fiona always said she could—and would—handle the situation herself. She didn't want anyone's help. Or their sympathy, either. She got defensive talking about it, and sometimes angry, so Finny rarely broached the subject.

Fiona blew a smoke ring above her head. "If you could go anywhere in the world, where would you go? Not just for vacation. To live, I mean."

"Stowe, Vermont," Finny said without hesitation. He'd gone camping there one summer with his father and Maggie, and they'd had a great time, hiking, golfing, swimming, sleeping in a tent by a fast-running stream at the foot of a lush green mountain. "It's so beautiful and clean and peaceful. I could *live* in a tent by a stream, I think. I've never slept so soundly in my life."

"What about winter?"

"Hmm. Oh. Well, I guess I'd need one of those tents people use in the Arctic."

"But you wouldn't be able to golf," Fiona pointed out, passing Finny the cigarette. He inhaled and quickly blew out a blue-grey cloud of smoke.

"Ah, well."

Truth was, Finny had lost interest in golf, a little. Over the years he'd won lots of trophies and tournaments, it was true (he was city junior champion four years running; a record at the time), but he wasn't having as much fun as he used to on the course. He disliked how competitive organized events were getting and how seriously his father took Finny's game. He felt pressured. The more tournaments Finny won, the higher Patrick's expectations became and the harder he pushed Finny to practice. And more and more lately, Patrick talked about Finny turning pro some day. At the very least, he told Finny, he had a very realistic shot at obtaining a full golf scholarship to any number of fine colleges in the States. The mere thought of moving made Finny uneasy. Besides, he wasn't nearly ready to think about college yet. He didn't even know if he wanted *to go* to college. Plus, he'd barely begun high school!

Also, there were crowds. They grew every year, the more Finny won. He disliked being watched. He would much rather play with two friends after dinner when the course was all but empty. They played for Cokes not trophies, and they'd swap clubs, putt with their drivers, drive blindfolded, and play trick shots off trees and ball washers and cart paths. When one of them pulled off a daring shot—skipping a ball through a water hazard, say, then off a bench, and back onto the green within ten feet of the pin—they would fall on the grass in a heap, roaring with laughter. *That* was when the game was fun.

Sadly, Finny was learning that fun, in golf as in most of life, was not always top priority.

Take school, for instance. Fun didn't even seem top priority in gym class anymore. After just one class, Finny had learned that sex education and basic anatomy would be taught in the classroom and there would be testing in the gym for some national exercise study, so that you'd be marked—in front of your classmates—on, say, how many chin-ups you could do in a minute. Finny was lanky and his arms were thin as hockey sticks; in sixty seconds, he wasn't even sure if he could manage ten chin-ups. He would die of embarrassment.

"Well, if I could go anywhere," Fiona said, "I'd go to Venice. Imagine being surrounded by all that water? You could take a gondola down the Grand Canal to wherever you were going—to a farmer's market or a quaint little coffee bar for cappuccino. How cool would that be?"

"Cool, I guess."

Finny took one last drag off the cigarette, tossed the butt on the sidewalk and ground it out with the heel of his desert boot.

"Not to mention all those romantic old buildings. All the beautiful piazzas and churches and palaces and museums. If I could," Fiona said, "I'd go there *now*."

"Wait, I thought I read somewhere that Venice is sinking."

"Blah! Sinking-sminking. If it were going to sink," Fiona said, "it would have sunk by now."

~~~~~~

Finny played the model student at Breckenridge for three years without a glitch. Maybe he *could* walk between the raindrops, he mused. Remarkably, in that time, he managed not to get called upon to read in any class, not *one single time*. In fact, as time went on, he began to feel less anxious and to enjoy high school. He made new friends, went to parties on weekends, got good grades, and made the senior football team as a kicker. Finny's great passion, though, was writing. The journals he'd filled in grade eight seemed silly to him now—at least the content did; when he read them over, he found they were full of puerile reflections and frivolous anecdotes. But at least he'd gotten into the habit of journaling. Midway through grade nine, Finny began keeping a "more serious" (his words) journal, faithfully writing in it day and night, whenever he found some spare time, be it a few minutes or an hour or more. He crammed his leather-bound journals, pages at a time, with more mature observations, things he thought were amusing, notes for poems and short stories, as well as his deepest, most secret fears and heartfelt thoughts. By the end of high school, Finny would fill more than sixty-five thick journals, using much of this writing in *The Orphan Diaries*, which would be published a week after his twenty-sixth birthday.

Finny's teachers praised and enjoyed his writing and encouraged him to write more. His stories were unusual, they said, yet unusually good, astute, mature. He wrote a story about a family who moved to the moon, about the life of a dining chair, and another about a man who made a fortune stealing tips from restaurants, enabling him to retire comfortably by the age of thirty.
~~~~~~

After reading "The Dining Chair," Mr. Caraway, Finny's tenth grade English teacher, became keenly interested in Finny's work. One morning he kept Finny after class and told him, "This is topnotch writing, Finny. It's clean, concise, bold, funny and honestly like nothing I've ever read before. I'd like to enter this in a short story competition, if that's all right with you."

"Wow," Finny said, but his first thought truly was: *Will I have to read it to anyone?*

But the answer to that was no. Thankfully. Mr. Caraway explained Finny had already done his part by writing it; all Mr. Caraway needed was Finny's permission to enter it into the competition. In fact, Mr. Caraway would mail it for him.

"So, what do you say?" Mr. Caraway asked him.

"Sure. Yes," Finny said. "Great!"

The competition was province-wide for high school juniors. More than four hundred entries were accepted and read by a jury of four professional writers. Three weeks later, in early November, 1984, word came that Finny had won. Excited and proud, Mr. Caraway plucked Finny out of his accounting class and, in the hallway, handed him the letter from the competition committee. It began: *Dear Mr. McKee: On behalf of the Ontario Secondary School Short Fiction Competition Committee, I am pleased to inform you that we have chosen "The Dining Chair" as the winner in the Junior Short Fiction category for 1984.*

"They called me 'mister,'" Finny said.

Mr. Caraway laughed. Then he said, "Congratulations."

A smile slowly grew on Finny's face, widening in increments, as he took the words to heart. He felt light, as if he might lift out of his Vans and float up into the air, and his fingers began to tingle. He leaned back against a locker and slid down it into a squat. "Holy shit. I won," he said, although the words seemed to come from someone else, some*place* else, far away.

"You did, indeed."

"Wow. I can't believe it. This is ... awesome."

"And you'll be a published author as well," said Mr. Caraway.

"What?"

Finny scanned the rest of the letter, which was brief, but explained that, for winning, Finny would soon receive a plaque, a one-hundred dollar bookstore gift certificate, and his story would be published in an upcoming anthology with nine other top stories from the competition.

At a loss for words, he ran a hand through his shaggy hair. He was shocked and overjoyed. His hands were all but trembling. He felt—what was the word?—*electrified*. That was it. Like electrical currents were pulsing through his system.

He had to find Fiona and tell her.

He sprang to his feet, hastily shook Mr. Caraway's hand, and told him, "I don't know what to say ... but thank you." Then he rolled up the letter and jogged off down the hall, his sneakers squeaking on the sticky tile flooring with every leaping step. Near the front offices he nearly lost his footing—he had to vault over the outstretched legs of two girls who were chatting on either side of the hallway—but he managed to keep his balance as he turned the corner and sprinted through the main lobby.

"Hey!" said one of the girls. "Watch it. Geez."

Over his shoulder, panting, he called back, "Sorry."

It was only after he'd run about a hundred more feet, passing by a Coke machine near the tech wing doors, that Finny realized he was heading in the wrong direction—but he was so thrilled, so bubbling with excitement, he just grinned and kept on running.

He was wildly happy about winning an award for his writing. It felt different than winning a golf tournament. In *The Orphan Diaries*, Finny wrote: "Winning that competition was validating to me and deeply rewarding on a very personal level. It was only then that I realized I wasn't just good at *playing a game*, which came quite naturally to me; and I wasn't just acting the class clown or playing a role, but I was good at something. Genuinely. I was a good writer."

$\sim\sim\sim\sim\sim\sim$

Finny had a crush on a girl named Megan Cook. She sat next to him in grade eleven history with Mr. Strong, a pale, silver-haired, angry-faced man who was rumoured to have once bounced a kid's head off a typewriter. (He also taught typing.) So, this certainly wasn't a class Finny fooled around in. Still, he talked to Megan every chance he could get. While Mr. Strong had his back to the class, writing notes on every blackboard in the classroom (there were four), Finny leaned toward Megan and whispered, "Why are we studying Jack the Ripper?"

Megan shrugged her shoulders. "I don't know. But it's kind of creeping me out," she whispered back.

She was a neat, pretty, studious girl, who wore bell-shaped skirts, crisp white blouses, and ballerina flats. Her short brown hair was held in place by a silver barrette in the shape of a butterfly. It looked old, like it belonged to some long ago era. Finny thought it might be an antique. Or a treasured heirloom handed down by her grandmother, or something? He'd been meaning to ask about it. Finally, one day after class, he did.

"It belonged to my great aunt," Megan told him. "A soldier

she was dating bought it for her as a gift before he went off to fight in World War Two. That's about all I know about it."

"Hmm," said Finny. "That's romantic."

Then Megan thought of something else. She said, "When she passed away—my Great Aunt Ellie, that is—my mom found a note left in Aunt Ellie's jewelry box saying that she wanted me to have it. I'm not sure why; she only knew me as a baby. And I didn't know her at all."

"That's fascinating," Finny said. He meant it, sincerely. "What happened to the soldier?" he wanted to know.

"Oh," said Megan, lowering her eyebrows. "I think he was killed."

"Wow." Finny cleared his throat. He said, "I mean 'wow' in the sense that that's sad and romantic and sweet. A beautiful story kind of 'wow,' I mean."

Megan smiled. "I knew what you meant," she said.

They walked slowly down the hallway. Students rushed by them on either side, heading every which way, making lots of noise. Some peered into their lockers. Others stood in circles, and talked and laughed. Finny asked Megan what she was doing for lunch.

"Eating," she said teasingly, and when she smiled, Finny could tell, she held back a laugh.

"Ha ha," he said. "What I meant was: did you want to go somewhere and grab lunch with *me?* Go to McDonald's or someplace?"

"I knew what you meant," she said again.

Finny laughed. He felt energized and nervous. "Well?"

"Sure. Just let me put my books away and grab my coat."

"Oh—okay."

Finny was pleased with himself.

It was March, and outside it was unseasonably sunny and

warm, with just an inkling of a breeze. Megan wore a sensible yellow rain coat, the zipper undone. She walked along the sidewalk with her hands in her coat pockets, her head held very level. Finny, meantime, was all movement. Ducking and swaying. Kicking clumps of old snow into the muddy gutter. Tucking his hands into his jean pockets and then taking them out again. Spinning around and walking backward.

"So what do you do when you're not in school?" he asked her.

"Well, I work. Hang out with my friends. Listen to music. Shop. Read. You know," she said with a smile, "the usual things people do."

He hadn't expected her to be so candid. He liked her sense of humour, too. She could say something funny without seemingly trying to be funny. Finny found her extremely charming.

"Well, where do you work?"

"At Sears, in the cosmetics department. It's boring and I never get a chance to sit down, but it pays okay."

"Seriously?" Finny said. "But you hardly wear any makeup."

"Ha! I wear, like, three pounds of foundation."

"You do?"

Her cheeks were nicely rosy, come to think of it—and now that Finny was looking more closely. Although he'd thought that was just her natural skin colour. He told her as much.

Her nose crinkled up. She smiled again. Her teeth were gleamingly white. "You're certainly very frank," she told him.

"That's true. It's actually weird," Finny said. "I tend to say whatever's in my head when I'm nervous. I have this sort of ... nervous chatter habit. Actually, it's more like a disease."

"I can think of worse things," Megan said.

"What? Like if I swore like a drunken sailor?"

"That would be worse, yes."

"Or if I spit constantly?"

"That too," Megan said.

When they got to the plaza up the street, they decided to eat at Lucy's Diner, a plastic-and-chrome, greasy spoon sort of place.

"Are you seeing anyone?" Finny asked Megan after they'd ordered.

"Dating?" Megan said. "No."

"You don't blush, do you?"

She ignored that—or maybe he'd mumbled the words and she hadn't caught them. At any rate, she told him, "Well, I was seeing Charlie Winter, but we broke up before Christmas. Turns out he's sort of high on himself and has an awful temper. Plus, all he wanted to do every weekend was get drunk with his buddies and sit around listening to Led Zeppelin and Pink Floyd records."

"Ah," Finny said. "Tons of fun."

"Exactly." Megan rolled her eyes. Then, "Are you seeing anyone?" she asked him.

He was taken aback. He chuckled. "Me? No. I've never really been in a serious relationship."

"Oh. But I thought—well, I always see you around with Fiona Walters."

"Fee? Yeah, well, she's just a friend. Pretty much my best friend, in fact. We've known each other since we were kids."

"Oh, I see," Megan said. "Well, I just think she's a wonderful pianist. When she played at the Christmas assembly, I nearly cried. She's very talented."

"Yes, she is."

Also, it occurred to Finny, she would be waiting for him at his locker right about now, or combing the parking lot for him. Oh well. He hoped she wouldn't be mad.

Their waitress came, a short, round woman with a tumble of brown hair pulled back loosely into a bun. She set down their food: a tuna salad sandwich for Megan with a glass of milk, and a giant cheeseburger and a heap of fries for Finny, plus a Dr Pepper. "Enjoy," she caroled.

"Thank you," Megan told her.

"Thanks," Finny said.

While they ate, they talked about anything and everything, it seemed, with Finny asking lots of questions. Did anyone ever call her "Meg" or similar? (They did, it turned out. Some of her girlfriends called her Meg, and her parents and grandparents sometimes called her Meggie, though she was beginning to dislike how childish that sounded.) Did she have any sisters or brothers? (Yes, one older brother, Philip, who went to Queen's and took film studies.) What did she want to do, as a career? (She wanted to be a physiotherapist.) Finny also learned that Meg, which he began calling her then, liked Duran Duran, Prince, Tears For Fears, The Smiths, and Howard Jones (his favourite band was, by far, U2, but he also liked the artists Meg listed off, which was a good sign, he thought), and she was a voracious reader of "classic" Victorian literature (Jane Austen, the Brontë sisters, George Eliot, and so on); she loved documentaries, romantic comedies, was addicted to *Cheers*; liked to jog and play soccer, had travelled to New York, Paris, and Spain with her parents (who both worked at the Ministry of Health), and took bubble baths that sometimes lasted over an hour. Also, her grandmother on her mother's side was nicknamed "Booby Ruby" because her name was Ruby and, well, Finny could guess the rest.

Finny, meantime, divulged the following: His real name was Finnegan, though he hated it, his mother had died of a "weak heart" when he was ten, and his father owned McKee's

Department store. He had an older sister, Maggie, who he'd grown apart from in recent years (she travelled with her own circle of friends now, and worked a lot at their father's store), his favourite sport was golf, and he loved to write and someday hoped to make a living as a writer. He was the world's most devoted U2 fan, as he'd already pointed out, but he also loved Simple Minds, Crowded House, Springsteen, Dylan, John Lennon, Simon & Garfunkel, and lots more; his record collection was massive. Stephen King was his favourite author, although he read almost every book he came across, and he was particularly, and perhaps strangely fond of reading about female authors who'd suffered from depression: Sylvia Plath, Anne Sexton, Zelda Fitzgerald, Virginia Woolf, Dorothy Parker, and so forth. His mother had books by and about all of these women, and Finny read them in his spare time. He liked trying to discern how the authors' afflictions (mostly depression) helped shape their writing. Admittedly, he likely spent way too much money—and time—in used music shops, he hated getting his hair cut, shopping malls, heavy metal and syrupy pop music, along the lines of Whitney Houston and Sheena Easton, blah, blah, blah ... he rarely watched TV, liked John Hughes' movies, could play half a dozen chords on guitar, fancied a cold beer now and then, and had never taken a bubble bath in his life.

They had a great talk, all in all. Finny didn't even bother with his French fries. He talked so much they were cold when he got to them.

By the time they got back on school grounds, they'd all but lost their voices. Megan kept looking at her watch. Finny wished she'd skip class and spend the afternoon with him, but he very much doubted she would. So ... "Listen," he said, as they stood in the parking lot near the tech wing doors. "Maybe we could do something some time? See a movie ... or, I dunno, *not* go to the mall?"

"I'd like that," Megan said sweetly. Then, lightning quick, she kissed him on the cheek. Something fluttered in Finny's chest, and he opened his mouth to say something but Megan had already gone inside. He turned and watched her walk briskly down the hallway, and he couldn't see her face, of course, but he was fairly sure she was smiling the same dopey grin that he was.

Thus began a wonderful relationship that would last until graduation.

"It might have lasted even longer," Finny noted in his novel, "if not for all the boneheaded things I did in grade twelve."

Still, Meg was his first true love, and he would remember her fondly, lovingly for years to come.

~~~~~~

One night in early June, Meg's parents went to dinner and a movie. Meg and Finny planned to make love, a first for both. They had, they figured, three hours alone at Meg's house. Not that they needed three hours, but three hours seemed like plenty of time. They were cautious about birth control. Finny had three condoms, which he'd reluctantly asked the school nurse for; he'd been mortified actually, and once he'd tucked the foil packets into his canvas bag, he'd nearly sprinted out of her office. But still, it needed to be done; it was, as they say, a necessary evil.

As soon as the Cooks' Volvo was safely out of the driveway
~~~~~~

and ten minutes had passed, Meg led Finny by the hand up to her bedroom. They got in bed and kissed—for a long time. Maybe fifteen minutes.

"Are you sure about this?" Finny asked.

"Of course," Meg said. She was sure about everything she did. Finny found that a little unsettling—though he couldn't pinpoint precisely why—but comforting as well.

They undressed. Slowly, at first, and then, as their kisses became more passionate, clothing began to fly: Meg's blouse, her bra, Finny's belt, socks, jeans.

"I love you," Meg said.

"I love you too," Finny told her.

In their haste to apply it, the first condom broke—somehow. But the second one did not, and they made love. And it was strange and wonderful, awkward and painful and intimate.

Outside, the sun was still shining. It shone through the lacy white curtains in Meg's tidy room. Children could be heard playing in the street. "You're it!" someone yelled. "No, *you're* it!" hollered another.

Meg lay with one arm across Finny's bare chest. Finny stared at the ceiling, wondering about his performance, a childlike grin on his face. He felt immensely, wonderfully carefree.

"Would you like a glass of water?" Meg asked him.

"Uh. Okay."

"Me too."

They dressed quickly, even though Meg's parents were likely now just ordering their dinner. Downstairs, Meg turned on the television and made some microwave popcorn. Then she and Finny snuggled cozily on the sofa beneath a big old quilt made by one of Meg's aunts.

~~~~~~

"What in God's name do you think you're doing?" Mr. Bosworth asked Finny. This was in grade twelve, and Mr. Bosworth was Finny's gym teacher and football coach, a fun guy with a beer belly and a full brown mustache that turned down at the corners.

"Coming to gym class," Finny told him.

Mr. Bosworth eyed Finny, head to toe, and shook his head. Finny was dressed in last night's clothes, scraggly jeans and an INXS concert T-shirt. His curls stood out wildly, as if he'd just walked in from a wind storm. He wore dark Ray-Ban's and carried a bucket of Kentucky Fried Chicken under one arm.

Behind Mr. Bosworth, Finny's gym class was playing badminton.

"You reek like a pool hall," Mr. Bosworth said, his voiced lowered. "Are you drunk?"

"When did we start with badminton?" Finny asked. "I thought we were moving on to floor hockey."

He waved to Meg, who was now the prettiest girl in school, as far as Finny was concerned. Racket at her side, she looked back at him, unsmilingly, and a shuttlecock hit her square in the forehead.

"Oh, brother," said Mr. Bosworth. "Come with me."

He led Finny by the arm into his office and sat him down in an orange plastic chair next to a metal rack of basketballs. Mr. Bosworth sat down on the edge of his desk and sighed. Then he gave a little laugh. Not a happy laugh. "Jesus," he said to himself. Then he told Finny, "Okay, here's what's going to happen: I am going to forget that you just walked into my class
~~~~~~

drunk with a bucket of chicken, and you are going to go home and sleep it off. All right? And then we'll talk about this tomorrow. Just you and me."

"Tomorrow's Saturday," Finny pointed out, licking his lips. His mouth was dry as a bone; his tongue felt thick.

"Shit, Finny," said Mr. Bosworth. "You're not doing yourself any favours here. You know, technically I should march you straight to the principal's office right now and you'd be suspended—God, maybe even expelled! You realize that?"

Finny nodded. "I'm sorry, sir."

"You're sorry."

"I am. Also," Finny said, "I'm not drunk. Just hung over. My buddy Watts had to go to court today so we were out late last night—commiserating."

"Commiserating?"

"Yep."

Mr. Bosworth rubbed his face with both hands and made a sort of groaning sound. "Finny, you're a good kid," he said.

"Oh, brother," Finny said.

"So what you're going to do is go home, sleep it off, and we'll have a little discussion about this on Monday."

Finny opened his mouth to say something, then thought better of it.

"Good thinkin'," said Mr. Bosworth.

~~~~~~

That was the year Finny's life took an irreversible turn for the worse, if you listened to Finny's father. In October, Finny began a new job as an usher at a movie theater and started
~~~~~~

hanging around with a group of older, unsavoury friends. Each night after work, it seemed, they frequented seedy taverns or trashy pubs, or held their own party at so-and-so's apartment. Finny began missing school, too, his grades had slipped, and there were frequent complaints from his teachers. Some days he slept till noon, or later, having come home at some ridiculous hour, stumbling drunk and incoherent. Other nights he didn't come home at all. Patrick was livid. Heaven knew where Finny'd slept, or if he'd slept, though Finny typically told his father he'd crashed at a friend's place. For five months, the boy came and went as he pleased and Patrick had no idea how to deal with him.

After all, up until now—up until he'd met the bunch of rowdies he presently called friends—Finny had been such a bright, studious, respectful young man, filled with promise, sure to make something good of himself. His father had been proud of him. And Maggie, too. She was a delightful daughter (and had never so much as sipped a beer, as far as Patrick knew): mature, polite, well-behaved, with a small circle of nice friends and a steady job at an upscale women's clothing store. After graduation, she planned on attending St. Lawrence College, although she'd yet to decide on a major. Still, at least she would be *going* to college. The way Finny was acting, Patrick couldn't imagine he'd finish the twelfth grade, let alone be accepted into any self-respecting college. He said as much to Finny, on numerous occasions, but there was no sense talking to the boy; in Finny's mind, it was clear, he had it all figured out.

"I'm doing fine, Dad. Just gimme a break and leave me alone," Finny told his father, during what would be the last of their many recent arguments. "I know what I'm doing, all right."

"Is that a fact?" said Patrick.

"Yes," said Finny, "it is."

This particular argument happened in the kitchen on a Sunday afternoon in February. Patrick had just come home from a Chamber of Commerce luncheon. Finny had just gotten up, apparently—his hair was wet from showering, and he kept yawning—and was fixing himself a tuna sandwich.

"You're screwing up your life, Finny, is what you're doing. You're flushing your good reputation down the toilet, is what you're doing."

Finny groaned. He put two pieces of bread in the toaster. "I'm not flushing *anything* down the toilet."

"Well, what about golf?"

"What about it? It's just a game, Dad."

"A game you happen to excel at and used to love, son. If you got your grades back up, you would have five schools in the States willing to offer you a full scholarship, Finny. *At least* five schools! Maybe more. Doesn't that mean anything to you? People rarely get chances like that in life. Believe me."

"Okay," Finny said, disinterested. He retied the belt on his bathrobe and hugged his chest, as if he were cold.

"Oh, this is all one big joke to you, is it, Finny?"

Finny sighed and rubbed his eyelids.

"And now you're going to just piss away the opportunity of a lifetime because you've made some cool new buddies. Is that it?"

"Listen, Dad," Finny said, trying not to lose his cool. "I just don't feel the same about golf as I used to."

Which struck Patrick as ridiculous. All that talent, wasted. A free ride to college, wasted.

"So you want to work at a movie theater for the rest of your life?" he asked. "Is that the plan? Because keep on doing what you're doing, buddy, and you'll get your wish."

"You have no idea what I'm doing," Finny said disgustedly.

"No, half the time, I don't," said Patrick, "and that's what scares me."

"Oh, Jesus. Can't you just leave me alone?! I have a job. I make money. I go to school. What more do you want?!"

"You go to school? You're nearly *flunking out* of school!" his father said through gritted teeth. He loosened his tie. He could feel his cheeks burning. "You show up late. You miss half your classes. You act like a *fool* when you are in class."

"Oh, calm down," Finny said. "I'm getting by."

The bread popped up in the toaster. Finny put the toast on a plate and opened a jar of mayonnaise.

"Getting by," his father muttered. "Getting by," he told his shiny black oxfords. "That's what you want out of life? To get by?"

Finny didn't answer. He opened a drawer, picked out a knife, then closed the drawer with his hip.

"You think you know it all," Patrick said. "You know what would do you good? A stint in the Army. They'd teach you a thing or two about discipline and respect and hard work."

Finny laughed. "Oh, get real," he said. "The Army." He rolled his eyes. "I told you, Dad, I intend to write for a living."

"Ha!" Patrick threw up his hands. "Write what—greeting cards?"

"Stories, Dad. Novels. You ever been inside a book store? They're chock full of 'em."

"They're chock full of discount bins too, buddy-boy. Do you realize how few people can make a living by writing? Do you, honestly? Very few, I can tell you that. And most need second jobs to boot. Is that what you want?"

Finny said nothing.

"Just the other day a guy was handing out poems to people in the street out front of the department store, asking for quarters. You want to end up like that guy?"

"Maybe," Finny said stubbornly.

"Oh, stop being so pigheaded and drop the act, Finny. You're only seventeen-years-old, for God's sake. You suddenly think you know everything. Think you've got it all figured out, huh? ... And now you just want to stop and smell the flowers. Well, good luck, son."

"No, I don't know everything," Finny said. "And I'm not pretending that I do."

"Well, then, listen to reason, for Christ's sake! Give your head a shake!" Patrick hadn't meant to holler. But he couldn't help it; his frustration was boiling over. He shook his own head. Wearily. He sighed and rubbed his temples. "Listen, Finny," he said. "I was seventeen once myself, you know—"

"Enough," Finny cut him off. He set the butter knife on the counter. Loudly. He looked out the window and heaved a tremendous sigh of his own, his shoulders slumped. "Enough," he said again, more to himself this time. He turned and marched by his father. Then he headed up the stairs, two at a time.

Several minutes later, he was back, wearing a brown leather car coat Patrick had never seen before, with his bulging canvas bag slung over one shoulder. He strode purposefully toward the front door.

"Where do you think you're going?" his father asked him.

But Finny didn't stop to answer. Without looking back, he opend the front door and walked out. The door closed quietly behind him.

Later that day Patrick showered, downed three aspirins with a glass of orange juice for the headache he felt coming on, and lay down in his bed to take a nap. His nerves were shot.

At six o'clock, Ana came to wake him for dinner. She knocked on his door but he did not respond. She called his name, but again, there was no response. She stepped into the room and stopped short. He lay on his left side, toward her, only his head visible above his maroon comforter; his face was very pale, his eyes wide open and still and lifeless. Instinctively, Ana stepped back, gasped and clutched her chest. For a long moment, she seemed unable to move. A fearful wail escaped her. Then she ran out of the room and down the hall to the office to call for an ambulance, even though she knew it was too late.

Book Two

The Neediest Person on the Planet

WOMEN LEAVE ME. They fall deeply in love with me and then they leave me. Eventually, perpetually, and typically after about a year. They say I am a scared, spoiled little boy trapped inside the body of a man. And once they come to this unsettling realization—baffled, frustrated, disappointed —they pack their things and shake their heads at me, and I rarely hear from them again. When it comes to women, I have never been a man of good fortune.

And now, on a blustery, sunny Wednesday in early April, it's Cicely, my girlfriend of thirteen months, who is leaving me. Well, more accurately, she's my *ex-girlfriend* and she's *already* left me—dismantled my heart, packed her things and had them moved to her girlfriend's place across town weeks ago, but she's forgotten an Oriental vase of some sentimental value, she claims, and she's come to my apartment to retrieve it.

"What vase?" I ask her calmly, though I'm extremely nervous. My inner organs feel like they're rearranging themselves. I wasn't expecting her; I wasn't expecting anyone, but least of all Cicely. When I heard the doorbell, I'd thought it might be Tim, the pudgy-faced kid from Scrubbie's who picks up my laundry. But it's a only few minutes past noon and he usually stops by after four.

"You know the vase," Cicely says.

"No, I don't."

I have absolutely no recollection of any vase, but then again I have a frustratingly fickle memory. Plus, my apartment is massive—in square footage, it's approximately half the size of a Canadian football field—and though it's not entirely untidy, it's cluttered with furniture, both new and vintage, and masses of mostly needless knickknacks. It's one of those huge loft apartments you'd see spread out across the pages of a glossy lifestyle magazine—all buttery wood, natural lighting, and exposed limestone walls—an occasional crash pad for a rock star or a jet-set model, say. But the thing is, I collect things. It's sort of an addiction, really. I'm crazy for castoffs and all things vintage, so I own positively way too much stuff: Philco radios, a fleet of pinball machines, arcade games, antique typewriters, cigarette machines, neon Coca-Cola signs, an Elvis decanter, a maze of age-old but pristine electric and acoustic guitars on stands, a model 1400 Wurlitzer jukebox, circa 1951, a full-sized snooker table salvaged from the tavern where Sir John A. Macdonald, Canada's first prime minister, was said to have frequented. Then there's the post modern pop art furniture— egg chairs, twin red marshmallow sofas, vinyl foot stools, blond wood box cabinets—and the inlaid, floor-to-ceiling bookshelves, overflowing with thousands of records, CDs, movies and, of course, books. So good luck finding a vase amid my carnival-esque blur of possessions—and I mean good luck on a *tidy* day. Molly Maid comes by every Friday to clean, but it's Wednesday, not a tidy day, and right now the old apartment looks unkempt and exceedingly crowded.

"It's tall. It's mostly white. It's very expensive. And it's in the back bedroom, I think," Cicely tells me.

"In a hurry?"

"Kind of."

"Right."

She is standing in the hallway, one foot on the marble, one foot on the Persian rug, as if she is not quite sure if she is coming or going. I am leaning against the wall where the living room meets the foyer, yawning, hugging my chest.

Cicely is beautiful. Empirically. In my estimation, it's not a matter of perspective. She has mesmerizing grey eyes that shine like the underbelly of a plane in the sun. When the light hits them just so, they can hypnotize you, if you're not careful. And her hair is long and lustrous, naturally blonde and curly—it hangs in tight, soft-looking ringlets and spirals well past her shoulders. Cicely is thirty-one but has the figure of a high school cheerleader: firm, wiry and curvy (in all the right places, if you ask me). Today she is wearing her favourite cream-coloured cashmere jacket, a short black skirt, and black knee-high boots. She dresses like this when she is in a good mood, or when trying to impress. I don't need to guess; she's clearly not in a good mood. She has a somber, concentrated look in her eyes.

"Well, come in," I tell her. "Go ahead and look for it, if you like," but Cicely just stares at me. It's a look I can't interpret. I'm wearing my Scooby-Doo boxers, brown mohair Kurt Cobain-cardigan, and pink fuzzy bunny slippers with half the right bunny's ear missing. I can't stop yawning. It's afternoon but I only slept three hours last night, tops, so I'm afraid I look rather rumpled. Having not yet showered for the day, I suspect my mad-scientist curls look their maddest. Cicely likes it when my curls look neat, or at least she did. I don't care—they do what they do.

"You still don't see it, do you" Cicely says sorely.

"Hmm?"

"When are you going to grow up, Finny? Look at you, you're a mess."

I look down at myself. "Well, I haven't showered yet and didn't get much sleep last night so—"

"No!" Cicely snaps. "Not how you *look*, you idiot. The way you are, the way you live. You're like a child, Finny, and you can't even see it!"

"I am not," I say, sounding, I regret, very much like a child. I sigh, suddenly feeling very sad. I have heard this before, from Cicely and other ex-girlfriends. I look around for a pack of cigarettes. Behind me, the kitchen table is littered with empty Heineken bottles and day-old boxes of Chinese takeout. I slap my thighs then realize my boxers don't have pockets. "I need a smoke," I tell Cicely. "Why don't you please just get your vase and go."

Cicely crosses her arms and steps forward purposefully. I shuffle back a few feet. The apartment door latches shut. "Because I want you to hear this," Cicely tells me. "Because I really think you need to hear this."

I think, *I really don't want to hear this.*

But Cicely says, "Finny, you need to grow up! You need to *wake up!* You need to stop avoiding everything and hiding behind your money. You really do. It's not healthy, any of it. It's pathetic, actually."

"Pathetic?"

"Yes. And you're pathetic if you can't see how pathetic that is. You're so needy, it's maddening! I swear, you're the neediest person on the planet. I mean, you're thirty-two years old and you can't even use the stove, for God's sake!"

"I use the elements—"

"You don't drive a car. You can't even iron a goddamned shirt!"

I sigh, heavily this time. To think: just three weeks ago I was madly in love with this woman. "Ciss," I say, in a more serious tone. She shifts her weight and tilts her head, as if to hear better. "I don't drive a car because I have the attention span of a gnat. You know—I'm afraid I'd be driving along and I'd see a herd of cows and go, 'Oh, look, cows,' then *wham!*" I slap my hands together; Cicely blinks. "I'd swerve and hit a fucking dump truck head on."

Cicely shakes her head, huffing. She narrows her eyes. "Oh, please, Finny. Spare me the dramatics."

"Dramatics? Ciss, I suffer from panic disorder," I remind her, slightly pissed off now, as well as sad. "You know—you may want to recall that. I'm *afraid* to drive."

"But you've never even *tried* it!" she says. "That's part of the problem: you don't try. And you're afraid of *everything!* Flying, crowds, movie theaters, the doorbell—it never ends. You want everything done for you—and you hideaway in this ridiculously massive, playpen of an apartment, chugging pills and drinking too much and feeling sorry for yourself. I mean, open your eyes, Finny. *Dammit!*"

Cicely exhales loudly, as if blowing away an ornery bee. Her bangs fly up. Her cheeks are flushed.

"I try," I say weakly. My fingertips are beginning to tingle, and I'm aware, all at once, my breathing is quick and shallow. "I do what I can," I tell her.

"And see!" Cicely all but yells, and actually points at me. "That's the really sad part, Finny. You can tell yourself that, but you have to know it's not true. You don't try; you never have. You cower and hide behind your money and anyone within reach. You have to see that you're lying to yourself. Please tell me you can see that."

But I don't say a word. Maybe there's some truth to what she's saying, but I'm not about to tell her that. And sure, maybe that is sort of sad, but I've heard enough, don't appreciate being barked at, and my nerves are frazzled. So I keep my mouth shut, head into the kitchen, and open the freezer to look for a pack of cigarettes.

I keep quiet because I know nothing I can say will appease Cicely, bring her back, or make her ever understand the dark, humming orbit of my fears.

~~~~~

I am badly shaken. Nerves frayed, an alarming knot of anxiety tightening high in my chest—like a sharp thread of string is tugging at my ribs—I light a cigarette and pace around my apartment. When I'm agitated, I chain smoke Silk Cuts, but right now I need more air. It feels like I can't breathe at all through my nose. (I have horrible sinuses.) And I'm beginning to feel lightheaded, too, so I drop my cigarette into a crumpled Dr Pepper can that's sitting on a bookshelf between a Brunswick bowling pin and my Charles Bukowski first editions, then head for the washroom, reciting my mantra: "This is just anxiety, it will pass, it always does. This is just anxiety, it will pass …."

My heart is racing and for a frightening moment I have this sensation that I'm falling, that the whole apartment is plummeting. I fear the pine floorboards will open up and I'll plunge down a dark, airless tunnel and be flung helplessly into the soundless vacuum of cold, smothering space. I put my hands on the walls to steady myself.

"Dammit," I say, and my voice echoes off the high, barrel ceilings. In the hallway I stumble over an old wooden milk crate filled with cassette singles. "Shit."
~~~~~

Then, quite suddenly, I'm afraid that I'm going to swallow my tongue. So I pinch my tongue between two fingers to make sure it's still in my mouth. Then, sounding like I have a mouthful of marbles or a severe speech impediment, I remind myself: "Hiss is uss ang-iety, ih ill ass, ih all-ays uz."

Then, again very suddenly, the light looks all wrong: unreal and grainy.

"*Sit!*"

A good dose of adrenaline shoots though my veins and my legs buckle, though I manage not to fall over. Tiny black and white specks fill the air.

"*Ammit!*"

I begin to perspire. Profusely. Sweat falls off my forehead and streams down my cheeks. I can hear the blood thrumming in my ears. "*Uck!*" I've abandoned my mantra. I pinch my tongue harder so that I can concentrate on real, immediate pain—pain that's not in my chest.

I need more air. I want it to be visible, like water from a shower head, so I can drink it in, gulp it down.

"*Od!*"

Finally, I stumble into the washroom, where I chew up three anti-anxiety pills—or "Crazy Pills," as I often think of them—and down them with some lukewarm tap water. The combination tastes metallic and minty.

I feel almost instant relief; the pills are fairly fast-acting, so just knowing this helps. But my hands and feet are still tingling from the adrenaline pulsing through my system. Supporting myself on the sink, I try my best to steady my breathing. I inhale deeply through my nose, pause, and then exhale slowly out my mouth. After several minutes, this breathing method seems to help. I'm no longer gasping for air, at any rate.

I turn on a faucet and splash cold water on my cheeks and

forehead. When I dry off, I bury my face in the soft fabric of the towel, which smells wonderfully fresh, like sunshine, like a spring flower I cannot name. I am not in any physical danger, I tell myself. The anxiety is unpleasant, but it will pass. It *is* passing. It always does. Thank heavens.

I stand up straight and take in a deep breath, and this time it comes much more naturally. The black and white specks are gone; so are the phantom pains in my chest. I've averted the worst of the panic attack, it seems. I close my eyes and let out a really deep breath, silently cursing Cicely.

But I resolve to let it go. Think of something else. Anything else. Toothpaste. C.S. Lewis. A band I once interviewed called I Bleed Gravy.

A cold beer will help, I decide.

Now I know full well no principled physician in the world would advocate chasing 6 mg of clonazepam with a bottle of suds, or three or four (whatever it takes), but in my current state I don't care. I truly do not. I've been through this hundreds of times before, and I know what works for me. I've dodged a full-blown panic attack and am headed down the hill toward calm. A beer will help cement me there. Not a bubble bath or deep abdominal breathing, or meditating to a Solitudes' CD, like countless self-help books about anxiety preach, but a cold, refreshing bottle of Heineken.

It's brighter in the kitchen. Sunlight streams through the sloped, pebbled skylight. There is nothing in my refrigerator but condiments, a dozen cans of Dr Pepper, Swiss Chalet leftovers, a squashed loaf of Wonder bread, and three neat little rows of Heineken bottles. I grab a beer and close the fridge with my knee. A chill crosses my shoulders and trickles down my spine. (I've still yet to dress properly for the day.) I take a corkscrew from a drawer, crack open the bottle, fling the cap clattering into the kitchen sink, and take a healthy swig of cold beer.

Then something brushes up against my leg.

"*Jesus!*" I howl, heart in my throat, and I spill some beer on the floor. But it's only Bowie, my all-black cat, twining his way around my ankles, looking for attention, tail sticking straight up. "God, Bowie, you scared me silly," I tell him. He meows at me twice. I can tell by the tremulous pitch of his voice that he's purring. He's fifteen, spry as a kitten, with a penchant for orange juice, peanut butter and Cool Ranch Doritos. Once he swallowed a penny and required minor surgery to have it removed. When I'm sad, he sleeps on my chest. I love him to bits.

I drink some more beer, though I'm still fearful I might swallow my tongue. It's this maddening tick I have; I can't seem to kick it. So what I do is allow myself tiny sips, one after the other, swallowing just a little beer each time, which, for some reason, causes me to belch a lot involuntarily. The belching earns me curious looks from Bowie, whose eyes are a charmingly content shade of yellow, like ripe corn.

"Sorry, Bo," I tell him. He blinks up at me disapprovingly, then meows again. "Yeah, yeah," I say. "Daddy's got to get a hold of himself here, then we'll have a tuna treat."

When I head toward my bedroom to get changed, Bowie follows close on my heels.

~~~~~~

Kicked back in a remarkably-comfortable zero gravity chair on the back balcony, I drink a second beer, munch on pretzels, and
~~~~~~

phone my sister. Selfishly—or perhaps not (she is, after all, my sister)—I need the distraction, and normally Maggie likes to talk. But today when she answers the phone, she sounds out of breath and there is a bunch of noise in the background. Voices, thumping, stomping; a tinny-sounding children's song coming from a radio or a television.

"Finny, I can't really talk right now," Maggie explains all in a rush. "Duncan's in the tub, T.J.'s throwing a fit because he can't find his favourite baseball bat and Johnny's in the backyard somewhere, though I told him not to go outside without sunscreen on—and Jora's got a piece of Lego jammed in his ear!"

"Oh boy. I should let you go then," I tell her.

I can hear my seven-year-old nephew Jora crying softly—not hysterically, as you might imagine—and saying, "No, Mommy, no." Then Maggie soothing him: "Come here, sweetie. It's okay. We'll get it out."

"No-*oh*," Jora repeats, in a whiny tone.

"Come here, please," Maggie tells him more firmly.

"I'll call another time, Mags."

"Well, no. What is it? Is it important?"

"It is to me. I'm really anxious. I just need someone to talk to for a bit and—"

"T.J.!" Maggie shouts. "Do me a favour please and check on Duncan in the bathtub. Thank you, sweetie." Then she tells me, "Sorry. Listen—just take a warm bath. Drink some herbal tea. Or go for a nice, long walk or something."

"I don't drink tea, Mags, and I don't feel like going for a walk, and you know I hate baths."

"Well, I don't know what to tell you, Finny. Just try to relax. Read a book. Jora, honey, stop *wiggling*."

I sigh and shut my eyes. People who have never suffered a

panic attack are always saying things like "Just try to relax." It is impossible, in my experience, to relate to them just how foolish that advice sounds when you know what it's like to be all but crippled by fear. But Maggie means well, I know, so I say, "Thanks." Then: "Maybe I could talk to one of the boys?"

But then there is some kind of crashing sound on Maggie's end, and Maggie yowls and says something hastily, which I can't quite make out, and hangs up.

So much for that idea. I click the off button on the cordless phone and set it on the circular cedar table next to me.

I swig my beer and bite down on a pretzel. A soothing Cowboy Junkies' song is playing on the stereo inside. (The CD is a mix of mellow, relaxing songs, a tool I use for just such occasions.) I light a cigarette and exhale with an approving moan. I've changed into a pair of tan walking shorts, a timeworn T-shirt, and my most comfortable shoes, brown leather Fender sneakers. The sun is shining brightly now, pouring down warmly on my face and shoulders, although it's still a tad breezy out, especially up here on the third floor.

The pills have kicked in, I'm sure—my breathing is normal, my thoughts are no longer racing—and I'm starting to feel a welcome little beer buzz. I think, *This might not be such a bad day, after all,* then swallow another mouthful of beer.

Below my balcony is a charming, tree-filled courtyard, long ago meant for horses and buggies. Now it's a maze of cobblestone alleyways snaking their way through a coterie of stately old limestone buildings, leading to this downtown street and that. I watch a woman in a grey wool dress pushing a yellow three-wheeled stroller at a leisurely pace, and nearby, an impossibly tanned, elderly man in a brown suit reading a folded newspaper under the shade of a towering spruce tree. As the woman passes the elderly man, he looks up from his paper and offers a courteous little nod and grin. The woman returns his smile and says something I can't hear. Likely something about the weather. The old man nods again, then returns to his paper.

This brief exchange of pleasantries helps bolster my theory that, for the most part, people are innately kind.

I smile around my cigarette, pick up the cordless phone and call my best friend, Fiona, at the bookshop where she works. The phone rings six times before she finally picks up and says, "Good afternoon, Bookendz. Fiona speaking."

"Hey, it's me. Busy?"

"Hey me," Fiona says gaily. She is a naturally exuberant person, although it's true she is prone to indiscriminate mood swings. "No, I'm not busy. Actually, I was just in the back skimming through this book about a woman who claims she went to hell during her near-death experience and spoke with Hitler."

"Oh, good for her."

Fiona giggles. She's one of those people who laughs through her nose, producing a sort of sniffle-laugh. I think it's sweet. "She swears on stacks of Bibles it's true."

"Oh, I believe her," I say. "What fun! I'm envious in a way. I mean, what great material for a book."

Fiona laughs again, then says, "So. What's up?"

"Ah ... not much." I drink some beer, hem, haw. "Although, well, Cicely stopped by earlier," I say.

"*What?!*" Fiona yelps.

She also has a tendency to overreact.

I don't know why but I feel oddly compelled to tell Fiona pretty much everything that happens to me. And so I do; I tell her every detail I can recall about Cicely's unpleasant visit.

Fiona's quiet a moment. Then, emphatically, she tells me, "She still cares about you."

"What?"

"Women are like that, Finny. We'll squash your heart like a bug beneath our shoes but we're never totally satisfied unless we know you're really, truly suffering. Then when we know you really are suffering and that you still care, we'll rub salt and vinegar in your wounds for good measure."

"Lovely," I say.

"She just wanted to make sure you were hurting, that you miss her horribly and are falling to pieces without her," Fiona says. "Trust me, women are mean as snakes. The vase was just an excuse."

I'm used to this; Fiona is one for grand pronouncements. And for a moment I wonder if she's even included herself in the "women" category—if she, too, is mean as a snake.

"Maybe so," I tell her.

Then Fiona tells me she should go. Her boss just walked in the door.

"Oh. Well, *wait!*" I say. "Are you playing anywhere tonight?"

"No."

Fiona is a career musician, a very talented pianist with a beautiful voice. She plays at bars and bistros and restaurants around town three or four nights a week. The bookshop is just a part-time gig to help pay the rent.

"Let's meet up later at Fitzgerald's then."

"Yes, we can certainly do that for you," Fiona says so sweetly she could spit sugar cubes. Her boss must be right there. "Is there anything else I can help you with?"

"Around six?"

"Yes, we close at five-thirty on weekdays."

"Great," I say. I'm genuinely pleased. Then just for kicks I say, "Hey, what's the difference between a pub and a clitoris?"

Fiona laughs a little, one tiny sniffle. "Um ... I'm not sure."

"Most men can find a pub," I tell her.

She laughs in earnest this time, four all-out sniffles. "All right, then," she singsongs. "Thank you. Goodbye now." She hangs up.

~~~~~

I've run out of pretzels, so now I'm snacking on fortune cookies. They're a bit sugary for my taste, but I love reading the messages inside: the vague predictions, irksome clichés and kitchen sink psychology. The first one I open says, "Your eyes will soon be sparkling. Keep them open."

I let out a bark of laughter. It's startling to think that someone, somewhere might actually get paid to write these things. Though, hey: not a bad gig, if you can get it.

The next one reads: "Pursue your dreams militantly."

"Militantly," I tell Bowie, who's sniffing the tip of my left shoe, completely uninterested. "I will hire a small army to help me pursue my dreams, Bo," I tell him. His response is to roll over on the deck and start rubbing his whiskers against my shoe.

I crack open another cookie, read the fortune aloud. "This is a really lucky day. Congratulations!" I sigh, toss the cookie over my shoulder, shake my head. "Lucky day, my ass," I grumble.

I should have better stood up for myself; I should have defended myself *militantly*. Because it's true: I am way too easily distracted to drive a car, and slightly clumsy to boot. There is absolutely no doubt in my mind that if someone were foolish enough to issue me a driver's license, and if I were to actually get behind the wheel of a car, I would mow down sidewalks
~~~~~

filled with people—a bunch of nuns or a class of kinder-
gartners on a field trip.

Is that so difficult to understand?

As for using the stove, well, that's just plain silly. I have
never learned to cook, and I don't wish to learn how to cook. I
like to dine out or order in. So Cicely likes to cook. Is that my
fault? Does that make me the bad guy? I mean, does anyone
seriously care if I only use the elements to heat up a bowl of
soup or boil some hot dogs? There are people who love to cook
(yes, I know there are people like this in the world, like Cicely,
like my sister—*oh, the pleasures of making homemade soup from
scratch!*), and there are people who do not. I am one of the latter,
clearly, and I don't think it should be held against me as a
character flaw.

And here's my stance on doing laundry: what a monumental
waste of time! I'm a Wash 'n' Fold kind of guy. I patronize my
local laundry service. Proudly. Some people like hanging out in
laundromats, reading a book or mingling with strangers while
their clothing spins round and round in the wash, but I am not
one of them. (Cicely was. She also claimed to enjoy ironing her
clothes, and loved putting on a pair of toasty pajamas fresh
from the dryer.) Call me lazy, tell me I'm wasting my money—
or both, as Cicely had more than once—but I am firmly
unapologetic about my stance on laundering. If you have the
means, let someone else take care of it. Why waste your time?
Simple as that.

~~~~~

We met in a bookshop. Fresh off a breakup, I was reading the
first few pages of C.S. Lewis's *A Grief Observed*. Cicely was
~~~~~

standing nearby, browsing titles in the Self-help section. Looking back, I might have known right then that our relationship-to-be would be doomed.

Later, we sat at tables near one another in the bookshops' café. I recall precisely what I was wearing because Cicely would later tell me I looked "sexy in a slovenly way": ripped Levi's, a black sweater so old the elbows were wearing thin, and a brown fedora with the front brim tipped upward. I sipped a massive hot chocolate and read my sad, uplifting book, while Cicely drank coffee and flipped through the latest edition of *Glamour*. But she wasn't really into the magazine; I could tell she was interested in me. Occasionally, she looked up and sent me quick sideways glances and flirty smiles. I am innately shy, so I worked to keep my eyes on my book, but after fifteen minutes or so of this cat-and-mouse, Cicely stood up, stretched out her long arms, yawned, and said to me, "That's some pretty heavy duty reading."

I glanced up. Nodded bashfully. "I guess it is," I said.

She was wearing a flattering red sweater, which made a big deal of her breasts, particularly when she was stretching her arms above her head. Although I tried my best to look at anything but her breasts—I examined my brown leather bracelet, looked over her shoulder at a clock on the wall, watched the young girl at the café wipe down the counter.

Cicely smiled easily, made a clucking noise, and said, "Yeah, well, I'm doin' some fairly heavy duty reading myself: planning the perfect beach day."

"Ah. Brilliant." I managed to smile.

Her hair looked radiant. I loved it. And having naturally curly hair myself, I knew her curls were natural. I also knew how soft those ringlets would feel between my fingers. She wore little makeup, had tiny lips, a sharp, pretty face, and her eyes gleamed like summer clouds reflected on water.

I was enamoured.

"It is," Cicely said. "See, if I skip greasy snacks and play some volleyball, evidently I'll get a great tan and have a fantastic time all the while toning my glutes."

I laughed. "Glutes," I said. I'd never heard the term, but I liked the sound of it. "Glutes," I repeated quietly.

Cicely looked at me strangely, like she'd just heard a kindergartner use a big word. "You've never heard of glutes?"

"No."

"Really?"

"Really."

I have always found it difficult to smile with teeth (at least around strangers) or, for that matter, to smile at all unless I'm laughing. Still, I tried my best to force another smile. I think Cicely could sense I felt uneasy, because she rolled her eyes and slapped the thighs of her skinny jeans with the palms of her hands. "Well, it's all silliness, really. Fashion magazines and all," she said. "Truth is, I'm bored out of my skull. All my friends go out dancing Thursday nights but I didn't feel like it tonight. I'm starting to really dislike the club scene. It's all wannabe hipsters and sleazy single mothers, you know?"

I did. I hated clubs. I said as much. Then added, "I'm definitely a pub kinda guy. I like to sit down, have a pint, talk to my friends and be able to hear them."

Then, as so often happens around strangers, my nervous chatter habit kicked in.

"I hang out at Fitzgerald's a lot. It's right near my place," I said. "Well, it's about a thirty second walk from my front door, actually. So, uh ... not far. And yeah, they have decent munchies, lots of good bands; it's a nice casual place. And the people who work there are really cool, too ... you know, they let you do your thing and they seem to know the precise moment you'd like another pint. It's great. I pretty much live there. Well, you know, not literally ... but it's a hang out." I cleared my throat. "But, who knows ... you've likely been there and I'm rambling on for no reason."

Cicely smiled. "I've been there a few times. I like their yam fries," she said.

"Right. They're good," I lied. I hate yam fries. I mean, they're *vegetables!* And if you ask me, vegetables have no place in the culinary world of pub fare.

"Hey," Cicely said, "I'm going to be going soon, but maybe you'd like to walk with me. I dislike walking alone at night."

I looked at her blankly.

"Or maybe we could grab an ice cream or something?"

"Oh," I said. "Uh ...."

I recall wanting to go to Fitzgerald's for a pint or two instead, but I couldn't work up the nerve to say so. My gut was doing somersaults, my thoughts racing ahead of me.

"I'm really not one for ice cream," I told her finally.

"Oh. All right." Cicely looked disappointed. Which made me feel like a heel. She began to gather her things, stuffing her magazine and a pair of sunglasses into a light blue tote bag the size of a suitcase. "I have a spinning class early in the morning anyway," she said. "But it was nice meeting you. I'm Cicely, by the way."

We shook hands. Her palm was soft and warm, her grip delicate yet firm. I imagined the rest of her was also soft and warm, delicate and firm. I got the shivers.

"Cicely," I said. "I've never known anyone named Cicely. What a beautiful name."

I was so nervous I was just talking nonsense, although it was honest nonsense. Okay, maybe it wasn't nonsense at all. Maybe it was the sort of honesty sheer nervousness induces.

"Thanks," she said. "It was my grandmother's name. My mom is really sentimental."

I thought about saying something nice about that, but instead heard myself saying, "Maybe you'd like to get a drink some time?"

"Sure," Cicely said without a moment's hesitation. "Let me give you my number."

I wondered how often guys asked her out. Likely all the time, I decided. I also found it odd that she didn't mention a boyfriend.

She took a notepad out of her tote bag. The paper was the same colour as her tote bag, actually, with pink flowers around the borders. With a flashy silver pen, she wrote down her name and number in a curly script, then tore off the sheet and handed it to me. "One of those is my cell, the other is my home phone. Feel free to call either," she told me. "I'm usually up until eleven week nights."

"Okay."

I examined the numbers. She'd even written her last name—Middleton. For some reason, that made me grin. I was still grinning, quite stupidly, I imagine, when I looked up and Cicely leaned in and kissed me on the cheek.

I flinched, nearly knocking over my hot chocolate (the giant cup wobbled on the table but stayed upright). I could feel my cheeks burning. And my heart beating fast.

Cicely smelled sweetly of strawberries. I remember thinking that, and also that she was very bold. I'd never met anyone so bold.

"You haven't told me *your* name," she said. She was standing too close to me, invading my bubble of comfort space. I swallowed. She smiled easily (with teeth), shouldering her bag. "You know, I should likely know your name if you're going to call me."

"Finny," I told her.

She nodded, contemplating that. "Well, Finny. I really like your hat. Call me soon."

I felt the brim of my hat. I wanted to say something but nothing came to mind.

Cicely smiled. And then she was gone, waving as she walked off and slowly descended the stairs, leaving me feeling bowled over and exhilarated, out of breath and genuinely, intensely, perfectly happy.

~~~~~

It's five o'clock, and I'm not entirely sober. But I've ordered in and eaten a Swiss Chalet chicken sandwich on a kaiser (heavy on the mayo), shipped my laundry off to Scrubbie's, and managed an anxiety-free, even blissful shower, considering how uneasy showering usually makes me feel.

I typically dread showering like a *normal* person dreads, oh, dental surgery. I'll chew gum, listen to calming music (two tiny high-end speakers are built into the washroom ceiling), and sit on the marble bench in my large shower stall under a steady, heavy stream of hot, hot water. Then, depending on the season, I will open the shower window overlooking the courtyard, and put my face to the screen, breathing in the real, cool air. That's the ritual, but most days the ritual only serves to eke me through the bathing process. Maybe it's being naked, feeling so exposed, or maybe it's the feeling of being enclosed—I don't know (and neither does my psychiatrist), but today, thankfully, it wasn't a problem. Two tracks off *Achtung Baby* and I was in-and-out and squeaky-clean in less then ten minutes, without a twinge of fear.
~~~~~

Now I feel great. Jazzed. Emboldened. A live version of Springsteen's "Born To Run" is spinning on the Technics turntable (circa 1978) in the music room and, via ten strategically-placed floorstanding, in-wall, and in-ceiling Bose speakers, reverberating magnificently throughout the apartment. I sing along in a raspy, Boss-like voice while dressing in my bedroom:

> *The highway's jammed with broken heroes*
> *On a last chance power drive*
> *Everybody's out on the run tonight*
> *But there's no place left to hide.*

From my walk-in closet, I choose appropriately casual pub attire: blue jeans, black T-shirt, chocolate brown suede blazer, and my favourite tan, corduroy cowboy hat, a well-kept 1960's Lanning, which I purchased online for $118 from a vintage hat shop in Wyoming. I slip on thin black socks then stand before my vast collection of footwear a minute before settling on a pair of Kenneth Cole boots, cut above the ankle, militaristic yet urban.

In the living room, I light a cigarette and check the time. It's five past five, according to the Rock Ola bubbler neon clock mounted on the kitchen wall, and so I call my friend Owen, who should just be getting off work. His cell number is easy to remember; the last four digits, perhaps not coincidentally, spell out the word ACHE. He answers after the third ring.

"Hey, Finny," he says. He yawns. "I'm just walking to my car."

"Okay. Well, when you get to your car," I say, "turn it on and drive on down to Fitzgerald's."

"Why?"

"What do you mean: *Why?* Why do you think?"

"Well, I dunno," he says apathetically. "It's been a long day and my back is friggin' killing me. Plus, I think I need new brake pads."

He's like this. A lot. A chronic complainer. He works for his brother-in-law on a survey crew ... surveying things. It's a job he hates, especially in the bitter chill of winter, but it pays his bills.

"I'll pay for new brake pads," I tell him. "And many beers, Owen—the perfect cure for back pain. Just come on out."

There's a pause. A car horn blares. "Let me think," he says.

"Don't think," I say. "Do."

"I dunno ... who else is going?"

"Fiona. And likely Julia, though I've yet to call her." And the Dallas Cowboy cheerleaders, he'd like to hear and I'd like to add, but I don't want to piss him off. Talking Owen into something he's not completely sold on is a subtle art.

Again, there's a pause. He's moaning internally. I can almost hear it. A car door slams shut. "What night is it again?" he says tiredly, as if he may collapse from indecision at any moment.

"Wednesday. Sad Bastards' Night. Half price nachos. Many attractive single female students. You know the deal."

After ten more seconds of annoying silence, he says, "All right. I'll go for one beer."

"Brilliant! Good man, Charlie Brown. See you in a bit," I say and hang up before he can change his addled mind.

~~~~~

Then I call Julia's cell. After three rings, I get her voice mail: "Hi. You have reached Julia Pritchard. Please leave a message. Bye!"
~~~~~

She sounds way too happy in saying goodbye, but I know she's rehearsed and practiced reciting the message about thirty times before nailing down this final version.

Thing is, Julia has a pronounced stutter, which comes and goes and causes her a great deal of anxiety. Sometimes it takes her ten seconds or so to get a word out, like there is a hitch in the gears of her vocal box. She is a very good and dedicated dietitian, but has trouble with some clients, she believes, because of her speech impediment. But she copes. Sees a speech therapist, a psychiatrist, an occupational therapist, and smokes copious amounts of pot.

There's a beep and I leave my message. "Hey, Jules, it's Finny. We're all going to Fitzgerald's a bit later on and would love it if you could come ...."

Then there's an ear-piercing shrieky noise, which temporarily deafens me. Bowie's ears prick up, and I have to hold the phone away from my ear. When I can listen again, Julia is saying, "Hello? Hello? Hell-oooooo?"

"Jules, hey. God! What was that?"

"Feedback or something," she says, laughing. Her laughter often sounds contrived but it's not, and I have no idea why that is. "I need a new cell phone. This one's had it. So, what's up? I didn't really ...."

There is a long pause. I wait patiently for Julia to complete her thought. I can't stand it when people try to guess what she is about to say next. It seems highly impolite, like staring at a person's glass eye or something.

"Hear," Julia says finally, and breathes a sigh. "Your whole message, I mean. Something about F-F-F-Fitzgerald's?"

"Yeah. We're going later—Fee and Owen and I. Can you come after work?"

"Let me think," she says, and then I can hear pages turning, and I can picture her inside her tiny office deep within the innards of Kingston Mercy Hospital—the yellowing walls and grey filing cabinets, the ancient desktop PC, the old scratched-up wooden desk, and the meticulously organized day planner she is now thumbing through. She tssk-tssks. "I have hot yoga tonight," she says, sounding disappointed.

"Hot yoga?"

"Yes. It's yoga in a heated room," she explains, in the manner of a pleasant elementary school teacher. "When your body is warmer it's more ...." There is a pause. I take a drink of beer. Stretch out my legs. "F-f-f-flexible. And because you sweat a lot, you rid the body of more toxins."

"Oh. I thought it was something else."

Julia laughs. *Hmm-hmmmp*, it sounds like. "You would," she says.

"Yes, I would. But hey—how long is hot yoga? I mean, is it an all-night thing? Maybe you could come after."

"Oh, I don't know. I'll be all sweaty and tired. It's really exhausting."

"So come out for a drink and unwind. Alcohol is an excellent muscle relaxant. Also, have some tasty nachos. Get some more bad toxins into you. You know, even things out."

"Ha! I'm trying to lose five pounds."

"From where? You're skinny as a rake."

"So *you* say. You don't get to see me naked in the shower."

"No. No, I don't, Jules."

"I'm getting a belly."

"*What?!*"

"I've a little paunch," she says. "And it's p-p-p-pissing me off."

"Aww. *A little paunch*. That sounds so cute. Like, 'I have a little friend.' 'I have a little hamster.'"

"Yeah, yeah."

"So, are you coming or not? You can drink water and eat lemons and cherries, then we'll toss around some darts for exercise."

"Well ...."

There's another pause, and I can picture Julia examining her cuticles, her mouth open, waiting for the words to come.

"I guess I could," she says finally. "Let me think about it, though."

"Well, don't think too hard," I tell her. Julia may very well be the most neurotic person I know. "Don't wanna pop a tube in your head."

She laughs again, but this time it doesn't sound contrived.

~~~~~~

We're at Fitzgerald's, an Irish-themed pub a chip shot away from my apartment. It's a cozy place, dimly lit, with a big old mahogany bar at one end and a stage and dartboards at the other. In between, there are tall oak booths and lots of Irish paraphernalia: football jerseys, Guinness placards, various flags, and oil paintings of Oscar Wilde, James Joyce, and William Butler Yeats framed in wood and glass.

Now—at six, straight up—the pub is bursting with students and regulars, but we've managed to secure our regular booth in the back, perilously close to a dartboard. Darts keep whizzing by our heads, hitting the dartboard in threes: *Thwunk! Thwunk! Thwunk!* Thankfully, the two men playing near us—with ties loosened and pagers attached to their belts—seem good and, perhaps equally important, fairly sober.

Still, "Why do we always have to sit here?" Owen asks, flinching a little with every *Thwunk!*
~~~~~~

"It's tradition," I say, and shrug my shoulders.

"It's dangerous," Owen says.

"Fine. It's dangerous *and* it's tradition. Cheers!" I raise my pint glass and take a healthy swig of Keith's. Owen shakes his head.

I haven't seen him in a week. His oily black hair seems a lot longer, though it's cut short in the back. His bangs flop violently to one side, hiding his right eye. His hair reminds me of Crispin Glover's in *Back To The Future*. It's a decidedly unfortunate hairstyle for today, but I keep this to myself because Owen is very sensitive about ... well, everything.

Like his Indiana Jones' hat, for example: a brown fedora he often wears and was wearing when he came here but took off the moment he sat down—like Fitzgerald's has a strict dress code or something.

Owen is really touchy about that hat. Thing is, it doesn't just look like the hat Harrison Ford wore in those movies, it is *one of them*. Owen bought it on eBay. I like to mention this fact to people just meeting him—you know, just so they realize he's a bit out there. It's gentle teasing, really, and Owen generally laughs it off, but you can tell it pisses him off.

But that's Owen for you: generally pissed off at the world. He's shy, self-effacing, socially awkward, and wound up like the innards of a golf ball. I worry about him. Recently he read a book called *Into The Wild*, about a college graduate who stops talking to his family, gives away his savings of $24,000 to Oxfam, and sets off travelling, eventually making his way to Alaska where he lives off the land for awhile but eventually dies of starvation. Owen loved the book and now he can't stop talking about it. And I have to admit that I wouldn't be that surprised to see him boot it up to Alaska sometime soon.

Now he's cupping his Guinness with two hands, as if it were a mug of hot coffee, waiting for the foam to recede. I suppose he's handsome in a plain way. His floppy Crispin Glover hair has its charms, and he has timid blue eyes, and a brawny, workingman's physique. He dresses neatly too (though boringly), in pleated, khaki pants and khaki shirts and big brown sturdy boots—even on weekends, when he's not working. He always looks ready to sail off into some thrilling archeological adventure, if need be.

Oh, he's not such a bad guy.

I'm thinking this when Fiona says, "I have a stalker."

She actually sounds proud. Like Owen and I are sadder souls for not having stalkers.

"Cool," says Owen.

"*What?*" Fiona says. "It's not cool, you bonehead. It's frightening."

Owen's face turns red. "Oh. Well, sorry."

"He meant cool like a video game," I tell Fiona.

"No," Owen corrects me. "I meant, it's cool someone's interested in you, at least."

Of course that's what he meant.

"Yeah, well, not this guy," Fiona says, shaking her head. "He's super creepy. Looks a bit like Jared Leto. He's greasy and pasty and clammy, and he wears black eyeliner. *Blah!* He tries to look all rock and roll but really he looks like he just crawled out of a scuzzy basement apartment and put on some cheap makeup."

"Sounds like a dream boat," I say.

"Yeah."

Fiona makes big eyes at me, like we're on the same wave length. She has playfully cheerful, expressive brown eyes. Fiona is quite pretty. In fact, a lot of people tell her she looks like a young Audrey Hepburn, with her black pixie haircut, sharp cheekbones, and petite, curvy figure. She guffaws at the notion, her cheeks turn pink and she covers her eyes like a shy little girl, but I know she secretly relishes the comparison. And maybe that's one reason she has a fondness for vintage clothing, like what she's wearing now: a simple yet elegant, slim-waisted, low-cut red dress, revealing a tactful amount of cleavage. I think it might be silk. And her shoes are black ballet flats, which, for some reason, I find endearing. Maybe because they've seen better days.

I should add, however, as a point of fact, that Fiona can sometimes look like a duck. She has an usually long neck and a long nose, so that when you look at her profile ... well, she can sometimes resemble a duck.

"Ugh. He gives me the willies," she's saying. "Big time. He dresses in sloppy black grungey clothes, like he was shot straight out of a Salvation Army store. Though he's got money. He works for the government. I think he's a computer technician or something geeky like that."

"Why is being a computer technician geeky?" Owen says, looking offended. Not only is he addicted to computer games and online dating sites, but he could dismantle any given computer and reassemble it perfectly in less than an hour.

"It just is," Fiona tells him.

Owen looks at me.

"It is," I agree.

He frowns and shakes his head.

"Anyway," Fiona says. "I remember this guy from a night I played at Pinkerton's last fall. He sat alone at the end of the bar and leered at my boobs for three hours. Then he bought a CD from me after the show and kept telling me everything was fantastic; my songs were *fantastic*, my voice was *fantastic*, the CD cover looked *fantastic*. He must have said fantastic about ten times, which I thought was annoying and peculiar. But I didn't think anything more about it until he started coming into the bookstore."

"Which was when?" I ask her.

"Last week. Well, no—once near the end of February and twice last week and then again today."

"What does he do—buy books?" Owen asks.

Fiona sips her vodka and cranberry, nods her head no. "Well, that's one thing that weirds me out," she says. "He doesn't ask about books; he just browses around awhile then ends up looking at the magazines. Then when he looks at me I'll say hello and he'll say hello back, but really he just stares at me and seems all ... *intense*. He's one of those people who looks at you like he's staring right through you. And he doesn't say much but he doesn't seem nervous either."

"Like Oswald," Owen says.

Fiona squints her eyes. "What?"

"Lee Harvey Oswald," I tell her. "Ignore him. This guy does sound creepy. What does he say to you?"

She sighs. "Well, the first few times he came in he said hello and asked me how I was, and how I'd been—you know, as if he knew me. And last week it struck me who he was and where I'd seen him before. But today was just bizarre. Today he just marched right up to the cash, brash as can be, and asked me if I'd like to go out some time."

"That's not so odd," says Owen.

"No," Fiona says, "but then he said, and I quote, 'Or maybe you'd like to come to my place and watch a movie.' And it didn't even sound like a question, that was the freaky part. Nancy was right there, too, taking an order on the phone. So I excused myself and said I had to take care of something in the back. I sat in Nancy's office for fifteen minutes and when I came back out, he was gone. Thank God."

"When exactly was this?" I ask her.

"About an hour before we closed."

"*Psy-cho,*" Owen singsongs.

"I carried a pair of scissors with me when I left work. I would have taken a cab if it was dark out. Yuck." Fiona lifts her shoulders and gives her head a little shake, like she's got the shivers. "I need another drink. Let's talk about something else."

~~~~~

Soon enough, after another round of drinks, we get to talking about Cicely's little visit. It isn't my choice, I can assure you. It's Fiona's.

"She's just got a wicked streak in her," she says. "She is naturally cruel—I always knew she was. She is one of those women who think they're beautiful and unattainable, so they think they can step all over men and it won't ever really matter because there will always be another one right around the corner. I hate that."

Vodka makes Fiona giddy and gripey, alternately. She's not too giddy at the moment. Though I wish she was, so I say, "Well, it's all right. I'm fine. I could care less what she said, really." Which is only partially true. "It's not like I'm contemplating the least painful form of suicide or anything."

Owen looks contemplative. After one Guinness, he claimed his back felt a bit better and he ordered another. Truthfully I think he actually likes being around people but refuses to admit
~~~~~

it. "I wonder what the least painful form of suicide *is?*" he says, pondering aloud.

"Pills," says Fiona, then hiccups a burp. "It's gotta be. Swallow a handful or two of barbiturates and fall asleep. Easy-peasy."

I wasn't trying to start a conversation about suicide. But hey—it is Sad Bastards' Night, after all. So I play along. I say, "Actually, I think it might be carbon monoxide poisoning. You know, park your car in a garage with the windows open a little bit, then just take a big long nap."

"I think a shotgun would do the trick," Owen says. "And quickly. The quicker the better, right?"

He kind of smiles. He owns a sword. It's mounted on a living room wall in his apartment. I sincerely worry about him.

Fiona rattles the ice around in her glass. "What about putting a plastic bag over your head? Some famous writer did that. He had inoperable cancer. Who was that?"

"Wait a second," I say. An old Rolling Stones' song is playing overhead: "Ruby Tuesday." A guy in a Red Sox ball cap nearby is laughing hysterically. Then all the people sitting at his table crack up. Darts go *Thwunk! Thwunk! Thwunk!* I have to raise my voice to be heard. "How would anyone even know? It's not like they could come back from the dead and tell some scientist all about it."

"Good point," Fiona says, and takes a big sip of her drink.

Owen bites his bottom lip. Makes clucking noises. "Still," he says. "You wouldn't feel pain for very long if you put your mouth around the barrel of a shotgun and pulled the trigger."

He looks proud of himself, like he's solved a difficult puzzle or something.

"I think I'll go for a smoke," I say.

~~~~~

I'm smoking in one of the limestone alleyways out back. Two attractive girls in expensive dresses and high heels pass by and one turns, smiles and says, "Nice hat."

I'm feeling pretty good, so I say, "Thanks. Nice dress."

They disappear around the corner, and one of them whistles. Then they both crack up laughing.

I smile, feeling even better.

The nearby courtyard is bustling with activity. Students are passing through in bunches, heading further downtown to one of the martini bars or dance clubs. They laugh and shout, drink beer from cans and stop to piss in hedges. (You can't walk down the sidewalk in this city without bumping into a cluster of students.) Two cooks from Fitzgerald's are sharing a joint beneath a maple tree. Near Fitzgerald's garbage shed, a teenaged kid in a red hoodie is playing "Sweet Jane" on an acoustic guitar for spare change. His voice is hoarse, and he won't meet anyone's eyes. He looks to be serenading the moon.

"Hey, Cowboy," someone says.

I look over my shoulder and see someone in the shadows. I walk down the alleyway, squinting, and see a man huddled on the ground, a blue blanket draped over his knees. He's wearing some sort of Army jacket, a few sizes too big for him, and a red toque with white stripes. He's handsome, cleanly shaven, though his eyes look droopy or sunken or something, like he needs some sleep. He has deep wrinkles around his eyes and similar grooves in his forehead. I'm guessing he's in his mid-fifties. A handwritten sign beside him reads: "Need $300 for dentures." *That's different*, I think. I wonder if it's true.
~~~~~

"Spare some change, kid?"

"Sure."

Cigarette clamped between my teeth, I take a handful of change from my coat pocket and drop it into the man's white bucket. The man looks into his bucket, eyebrows raised, like he's hit the jackpot.

"Thanks." He sounds genuinely grateful. I might have given him close to ten bucks.

"You really need dentures?" I ask him. This is something I would never ask if sober. But I'd wonder.

"Yes. I do," the man says in a scruffy voice. Then he opens his mouth and smiles; he's all gums.

"Right," I say, looking away. "Thanks for that."

"I get a disability pension from the government, but they only cover basic dental work," he tells me.

"That sucks."

"Yes. It does. It's a terrible system."

I take a drag off my cigarette. Exhale. I wonder what the man's disability is. I wonder if he has a home.

Then it hits me: a big idea.

"How long have you needed dentures?" I ask the man.

He rubs his eyelids with two fingers on his right hand, yawns. "Awhile now. Coupla years, I guess."

"Do you have a dentist? Or what is it—a denturist?"

"Yes, I have a dentist. Dr. Eastwood. No relation."

The man's eyes brighten and he comes close to a smile. I laugh.

"Listen," I say. "I have money. I mean ... I have money to spare. And I can pay ... I can help you get your dentures, is what I'm trying to say."

He looks me over a moment, like I'm nuts. Or maybe he thinks I'm drunk. Which I might be, let's face it. I would certainly fail a breathalyzer test right now, at any rate, but I know what I'm doing. At least, it feels right, what I'm trying to do. The man looks away, scratches his chin. I hope I haven't offended him. Though he does have the sign, right? He *is* asking for money.

"I'm not crazy," I tell him, in case he's wondering. "I mean, I may be a little drunk, but ... whatever. The thing is, I'm sort of wealthy. My father was wealthy. But he died when I was a teenager. So I inherited a lot of money the day I turned eighteen. And I don't usually talk to people about this, but your sign ... it's just, I don't know ... I'd like to help you. And my father was a good, kind man, really, and I know he would want me to. He would have done the same thing, in fact. In a heartbeat. No questions asked. Well, maybe a few questions asked."

The man looks up at me. Appraisingly. "How'd he die?"

"Brain aneurism."

"Hmm." He looks thoughtful. "What about your mother?" he asks.

"Pardon?"

"You inherited lots of money, you said. Didn't you have a mother?"

"She died when I was ten," I say. "Heart attack."

He nods, lowering his bushy eyebrows. "That's sad," he says. "I'm sorry."

"Thank you."

He thinks a moment. Looks at my boots. His eyes move up, down. He sighs. Scratches his chin again. Finally, he says, "It would be nice to have new teeth. Well, not *new* teeth. You know what I mean."

I smile. "I do. And we can do this however you want. You

could make an appointment with your dentist and I could meet you. Or I can go to a bank machine right now and get you the money."

"You'd do that?" the man says.

"Which?"

"Meet me at the dentist's office?"

"Yeah. For sure."

I like big ideas; they excite me. And I get them all the time. My heart is beating fast, but in a good way, not a panicky one. I am filled with an overwhelming sense of well-being, the sort of unassailable peace I long for every minute of every day but seldom attain. It's astonishing, how good I feel, how utterly content and unafraid. I'd almost like to sing about it. I am thinking clearly, very clearly. Somehow I feel compelled to help this man, though I can't say why precisely.

"Well, I don't have a phone," the man says in a hushed voice, as if speaking to himself.

"That's okay," I tell him. "You could just come by my place."

He gives me that look again, like I'm crazy or cockeyed. "I meant," he says, "I don't have a phone but I guess I can go on down to the dentist's office and make an appointment."

"Oh. Right. Sorry."

The man looks at his sign, then at his bucket. There are a couple of bills fluttering around in the bucket, but mostly quarters and dimes and the toonies I just gave him.

I hold out my hand. "I'm Finny," I tell him.

He looks at me. Then at my hand. He shakes it. His is cold and calloused. "Walt," he says. "Not Walter. Just Walt."

And maybe it's some combination of the booze in my system and feeling exhilarated by this big idea, or something else entirely, but I think it's the most gentle sounding name I've ever heard.

Walt.

So then I say, "You know what: let's make this easier. You need three-hundred dollars to get dentures? That's the exact amount?"

He nods that it is. "Give or take a dollar or two."

"I'll be right back," I tell him. I walk to Princess Street, then up half a block, and go to an ATM at the corner. I hit a few buttons, grab a fistful of twenties, and stuff them into an envelope. Then I retrace my steps and present it to Walt. "There you go," I say. "New teeth money."

~~~~~~

I am supremely happy. I haven't a care or fear in the world at the moment, and it's blissful. I have a full, cold pint, I'm with friends (I'm rarely happier than when I'm buzzing and with friends, even if they are curmudgeonly misfits), and all around us people are laughing and engaged in spirited conversations. Also, I'm sitting on a terrific secret and it's a cool feeling. I won't be telling Fiona about Walt. Not tonight. Or at least, not now.

We've ordered our third or fourth round of drinks (I've lost track), and a twenty-something girl in a multicoloureded poncho has taken to the stage—just her, a small Peavy amp, and an acoustic guitar, a beautiful, big-bodied Alvarez with a solid spruce top. She plugs in, taps the microphone, and then kicks into a song. I don't recognize it; it must be an original— something about love being a weapon of peace. She has a nice voice, gritty, with a little country twang. She's pretty without the aid of makeup, and looks like she might have been transported
~~~~~~

here directly from a '70s San Francisco peace rally, with her faded, bell-bottom jeans, long scraggly brown hair, and black cat's eye glasses. Though it's really the multicoloureded poncho that screams *hippy*. And also the fact that she is singing barefoot. Before I can ask who she is, Fiona says, "Holly Kidden."

"Wow," I say, and nod my head, a silly grin on my face. "She's quite ... wow."

Fiona rolls her eyes to the side. "Yeah, big wow. She sings like a little girl. She looks like a little girl. And what a stupid name—Holly Kidden. Holly ain't kiddin'. Holly likes kittens."

This is something I dislike about Fiona: she can be childishly petty at times, particularly about other musicians, and especially female musicians. They are her competition, I suppose, but other musicians I know around the city pull for one another; they're friends; they jam and play on one another's records; they belong to a hip, private community of struggling artists—and Fiona wants nothing to do with any of them.

"I like her," Owen says, turned around in his seat for a better look.

"Yeah, massive surprise, Owen," Fiona says. "She has tits." Then she looks back at me. "Wow *what*, Finny?"

"I don't know, Fee. She's good. She's very ... poised. That's one helluva guitar. And she is rather attractive."

"She's *gorgeous*," Owen agrees.

"She's a fucking *clone*," Fiona snarls, looking like she might spit venom or eat her teeth. "She's a Lisa Loeb look- and sound-alike, for God's sake. She's practically spitting up syrup. Am I the only one hearing this—what?"

I shrug my shoulders. I'm in no mood to bicker.

"If she's signed to a record label, I'll puke. But that's the sick thing: she's exactly what record labels want," Fiona says to no one in particular. "Blowzy young waifs with just a speck of talent who look like goth punks or wannabe flower children. It doesn't matter if they're over-the-top beautiful or plain as vanilla. As long as they're young, they can be transformed into high-end fashion models. Problem with me is, I'm too old and my ass is too big."

"You're not too old," I say.

She shoots me a squinty look, her eyes shrinking to the size of decimal points.

"And you have a nice ass," I'm quick to add. "Just the right-sized ass."

"Yeah, right. If I don't get signed by a decent label within a year, I will never play another show as long as I live. Not even for charity or folks in a nursing home."

I let her rant. It's best this way. Try to play up her successes and she'll only shoot you down.

Fiona says, "I'll donate Gertrude" —her electric piano— "to Goodwill and grow old without ever getting married or having children. I'll be one of those old spinsterly ladies who lives with a thousand cats, without ever having made my mark on the world."

I can't help myself. I say, "At least you'll have been loved by many, many cats."

This earns me a groan and an eye roll.

"Do you know how many CDs I've sold since January?" she asks me.

I shake my head. And I don't dare venture a guess; if I were wrong and guessed on the low side, she'd likely throw her drink in my face.

In January, Fiona released her first independent CD, *Cigarettes In Heaven*, which she produced and played every instrument on—mostly piano, but some percussion and bass as well. She even sang her own backup vocals. Locally, the record received some good reviews, and there was also a positive, though brief, write up in *NOW* magazine. Also, the first single—a bluesy, piano-driven cover of Dylan's "Stuck Inside Of Mobile With The Memphis Blues Again"—has gotten some play on CBC and college radio. But Fiona seems to think all the early and modest success won't last. When the novelty wears off, she's told me, her CDs will gather dust in record shops' cheap bins, and the people who've already bought a copy will end up using them as coasters.

"Two-hundred and two," she says. "Most of those I've sold at gigs, and half of those were bought by guys who just want to get into my pants. Meantime all these people send me e-mails on MySpace saying, 'Oh, I just love your voice. You're so incredibly talented.' And, 'When are you coming to Hamilton? We'd love to come out and hear you!' Well, skip your Fair Trade grande mocha light espresso goddamned Starbucks' coffee one morning and buy the fuckin' CD already!"

"What's that?" Owen says, but his gaze never leaves the stage. He's rapt, his eyes locked on Holly Kidden's every move.

"Oh, screw off," Fiona tells him. "I don't know why I bother. Playing to six people some nights, half of them employees. In taverns with out-of-tune pianos and pubs that reek of piss and stale beer. With students doing body shots and playing Quarters while I'm playing a ballad and singing my guts out. Why do I keep doing this to myself?" she asks me. Her voice cracks. She seems about to cry.

"Because it's what you were born to do," I tell her, like I've told her countless times before. "Because people love your music, Fee. Because you love to play and sing."

She begins to cry, soundlessly, and it breaks my heart. Sure, she's being petty and snarky, but she has every right to be angry at the world, Lord knows. Growing up with her mother was hell. It's truly a wonder to me, actually, that Fiona survived those years, hadn't gone mad and ended up institutionalized, or worse. Times like this it's impossible for me to look at Fiona without seeing that sad little girl I grew up with, bruised and shaking, a gash in her cheek, a cast on her arm—a frightened, fragile soul with dark, hollow brown eyes quivering with fearful tears. So I can never hold it against her if she is sometimes frustrating and abrasive. I love her like a sister, and I figure I always will.

I pass Fiona a napkin and she wipes her nose with it. I need to change the subject. Quickly. "That's a beautiful dress, Fee," I tell her.

"Hmm?"

"Your dress. It's gorgeous. Where'd you get it? I've never seen it before."

Then she perks up a little. Blows her nose and tosses the napkin aside. Wipes her eyes with the back of her hand and blushes, a hint of a bashful grin on her face. "Oh, this old thing." She sniffles a laugh.

I sip my beer and nod. "It's very Audrey Hepbern," I say.

"Actually, it *is* an old thing," she says. "Like thirty years old. I picked it up last week at the Gypsy Loft for twenty-one whole dollars. No tax."

"Nice."

"Very, seeing that it might be worth about ten times that."

"Really? Sweat deal."

"I had to work on a few seams, trim a few loose threads, but it was worth it."

"I'd say so. You look lovely, sweetie," I say. "Sincerely."

She smoothes over a patch of fabric near one shoulder, looking shy and proud.

Meantime, Holly Kidden finishes a song to a smattering of

applause, but Fiona doesn't seem to notice, which is good. She can turn on a thread. Next time I go for a smoke, I know she'll come with me and bum one, and we'll get silly and break out laughing and then she'll want to come over later and drink caesars, order pizza and play Ms. Pacman till 4 A.M.

"Hey. What do you think?" I ask Owen, but he's off in his own little universe, gazing at the girl on stage. He doesn't even say, "Hmm?" I nod my head—*little boy lost*—and Fiona meets my gaze and offers a knowing little head shake, like we're on the same page and Owen is in a different book.

"Fee," I say, to see if Owen is paying any attention to us whatsoever. "Did you hear they're thinking of making another *Star Trek* movie?

But no, nothing, zilch—no visible or audible reaction from Owen.

Fiona grins sweetly, playing along. "I did. I think it begins with Captain Kirk meeting Spock in rehab. It's more about the characters than the action."

"I also read somewhere that Nostradamus *predicted* they would make another movie."

"Wow," Fiona says. "Blah blah blah, Nostradamus, *Das Boot*."

"Yes. And George Lucas eats photon torpedoes for breakfast," I say. "Apparently they're quite tasty."

"Like Strawberry Poptarts," Fiona agrees, wrinkling her nose at me in a funny way. And we almost get to losing it laughing, when Owen turns his attention away from the stage, back to us and says, "Hmm?"

"Pardon?" I say.

"What?" he says, looking dopey and distant.

A sniffle-laugh escapes Fiona. She clears her throat. "Hey, how's the internet dating scene, Owen?"

He thinks about this and smiles mischievously. "Pretty good," he says. "Actually, I had a date last weekend."

"And?" I say. "Come on. Spill the beans."

"It went well," he says.

"Details, Owen. Details. The best parts of life are often in the small details, my friend."

"Yeah. What's her name? What did you do?" Fiona prods.

Owen nods his head and his grin widens. "Well, her name is Rachel, and she just came over to my place. We talked and listened to music and drank a lot of wine and then ...." He giggles. "Then someone phoned and while I was talking to them she got on the floor and sort of crawled over to me on her knees and started sucking on my fingers."

I laugh. "Brilliant!"

"This was a first date?" Fiona asks.

"Yep." Owen seems about to laugh, too.

"How can you keep this shit to yourself?" I ask him. And I laugh some more; I can't help it.

"So then what?" Fiona wants to know.

"Well. Then I hung up and she kissed me and ... okay ... put it this way—we didn't get much sleep after that."

"Fantastic!" I say, and pound a fist on the table for good measure, and get to laughing even harder. "Absolutely magnificent! Good show, Owen. Just ... good for you."

Owen looks incredibly pleased with himself, like a kid who just got the teacher to sit on the whoopee cushion.

But Fiona looks perplexed. "This was a *first* date?" she says again—incredulously.

"Yeah. Well, I guess. We chatted online a few times. Then on the phone. Then she came over."

"And drank bottles of wine and sucked on your fingers?"

Owen smirks. "Well, yeah."

Fiona shakes her head, baffled. "What ever happened to going to the movies? Or sending flowers and dinner dates? Whatever happened to *getting to know* someone before you jump into bed with them?"

"We got to know one another," Owen says, and he doesn't mean it in a dirty way, it's clear. He's being genuine. And I'm impressed by his sincerity, and also because he's defending himself against Fiona. Normally, she intimidates him. "And we're *still* getting to know one another," Owen adds. "She's really very nice."

Fiona takes a deep breath. I can tell she wants to say something else, something sarcastic or nasty, but she doesn't. Instead, she nods at the table, then takes a look around the pub.

It's busier now, and louder. There's a buzz of frenetic conversations, wails of laughter, and people shouting to be heard. Holly Kidden is finger picking an ethereal-sounding instrumental number, and a bunch of Queen's nursing students at the booth across from us are loudly talking shop.

"I'd rather clean up puke all day than give one single enema," the tallest of them says, the one wearing a Queen's hoodie.

"Eeew!" the girl next to her says.

"I'm serious. I'd rather work on neurology with all the masturbating goons with brain injuries. Enemas are disgusting."

"And the masturbators are any better?"

They have plates of food on their table: pub wraps, burgers, yam fries, onion rings. *How can they talk about puke and masturbating goons while they're eating?* I wonder.

"Oh, Lord," Fiona says, and rubs her forehead. "I weep for the future of our unborn children."

~~~~~~

I'm outside, smoking in the courtyard again, when I see her: a ravishingly beautiful bohemian goddess of a woman. She has a curvy figure, long, lustrous chestnut hair, bright brown eyes, and a startling smile. She is standing near the big green back door to Fitzgerald's with two other women—clearly her friends—and they're talking and laughing.

I'm drawn closer.

A cell phone rings. One of the other women produces a tiny pink phone from her clutch, puts it to her ear and says, "Hey! Where are you? We're just outside Fitzgerald's. Yes. We're here now."

The two friends are a blur to me, though; I'm staring at the woman whose curly hair tumbles in tousled waves over her bare shoulders. She's wearing hip-hugging cords, the same colour as her hair, a sleeveless white peasant blouse with a tiny blue butterfly embroidered near one shoulder, and flowery flip-flops. A teal scarf is wrapped around her neck. It's a casual, bohemian look I adore and have a decided weakness for.

I bet her name is Edie or Sasha or Sunshine. I bet she has a vegetable garden in her back yard. Eats granola and tofu and salads. Maybe she sleeps in the nude.

I'm about ten feet away from her now, standing here and staring.

"Forget about The Grizzly and come on down here," the girl on the cell phone says.

Then Edie or Sasha or Sunshine looks over at me. She smiles warmly. And winks.

My heart stops or skips several beats or something. I open
~~~~~~

my mouth to say something but no words come out, only a short, disbelieving laugh.

Then her other friend says something to her and she looks away.

Her nose is sprinkled with freckles. Her hair falls over her forehead in a sexy slant, covering up one eye.

I couldn't blueprint a more beautiful woman.

The friend with the cell phone wanders off, saying, "Stages? *What?* Speak up. I can barely hear you."

The other friend follows. She says, "Marnie, did you say Stages? No way in hell I'm going to Stages."

I walk up to Edie or Sasha or Sunshine. "Hi," I say. "I don't want to bother you but I thought ... Did you just wink at me?"

She smiles. There are tiny laughs lines around her mouth. She has pale, soft-looking skin. "I smiled at you," she says. "But I didn't wink at you."

"Oh. Well. I thought you did. I really thought you just winked at me."

"Nope," she says. "I didn't. I do wink sometimes, though."

I love her voice. It's feminine, but a little bit husky. It's warm and soothing; it calms me.

"Right," I say.

Then I can't think of a thing to say. I drop my cigarette to the ground and crush it beneath my boot.

"I like your hat," she tells me.

"Oh. Thank you. I collect them."

"It's cool. Distinct."

"It's also dangerous," I say. "Drunk people sometimes have a problem with it, that is."

"Well, you're a brave soul then."

I laugh. "I guess so."

She pushes back her hair. Her eyes are luminous, lively.

Then one of her friends hollers, "Kathleen, we're going!"

"Okay," she says.

"Wait!" I say, a little too loudly. Kathleen pulls back and laughs at me. "Sorry. I mean ... um ... before you go. Well, maybe you'd like to get a drink some time? Or, I don't know, do ... something."

"Sure," she says brightly. "I'd like that. Got a pen?"

"What?"

"I was going to give you my phone number."

"Oh, right. Yes, I do."

I fumble around in my coat pockets. I always have a pen on me. (Other things I always have on me: a small Reporter's Notebook, Halls, gum, a Vicks inhaler, a bottle of Crazy Pills, and my cell phone. If I go out and forget any of these items, I get all panicky.) Eventually, I find the pen. I tear out a sheet of paper from my Reporter's Notebook, and hand Kathleen the pen and paper.

"You're all prepared," she says. "How cute."

"Well, no. It's not for that. I'm a writer, I mean. I take notes all the time," I say. I'm afraid I sound like a bumbling moron.

But Kathleen seems amused by me. She's been smiling this whole time. My guess is she's in her late twenties. Although she might be older. It's difficult to tell.

"I'm Kathleen," she says, giving me back my pen and the sheet of paper.

"I know," I say. "What I mean is, I heard your friend call your name."

I do: I sound like a bumbling moron.

"And you are?"

"What? Oh. Finny. I'm Finny."

She laughs again. "Cool hat *and* a cool name," she says, nodding her head, smiling her wonderful smile.

Then there's a moment when I think she might say something else. But she doesn't. Like she doesn't feel the need to fill the empty space. I like that.

"*Kathlee-een!* We've called a cab," her friend calls over. "Come on, sweetie."

"Coming," she says. Then to me she says, "So I'll talk to you soon, I guess. It was nice meeting you."

"You too," I say.

Her friends are giggling. They take her by the arms, lead her away, and start talking at the same time. Then Kathleen turns and says, "Call before ten, though. Okay?"

"Okay," I say.

They walk arm in arm by a group of older guys, who are smoking by the bench where I saw the impossibly tanned elderly man sitting much earlier. The guys' heads swivel. One of them whistles—a cat call. But Kathleen and her friends ignore them. They laugh and disappear down one the alleyways.

I slip the pen and paper in a pocket. Then I head back inside, smiling to myself, happy as sin.

~~~~~~

I dream I'm seated on an airplane next to Cicely. The plane is large—a 747, likely—but I am unaware of any other passengers. We are flying smoothly over a mountain range, green fields in the distance, blue sky all around.

"But you're afraid to fly," Cicely says to me. She is wearing all pink: a short skirt, suit jacket, even a pill box hat, like Jacqueline Kennedy wore the day her husband was assassinated.

"I am," I tell her. "I'm absolutely petrified. I doubt I'll *ever* fly."
~~~~~~

Cicely shakes her head at me and looks out her window. She says, "You can't come with me, you know. It's for the best."

"But where are we going?" I ask, my voice sounding croaky, like I've just woken up.

Cicely shrugs her shoulders in an uninterested manner. Then, "Look!" she says. "There's your mother, painting on a cloud. I thought she was dead."

I am unable to speak. The word "mother" sounds unrelated to me, like a word in Spanish or German I do not know. Then, suddenly, the plane takes a steep dive. It shakes from turbulence, causing our seats to vibrate violently. Cicely's hat falls off. Luggage rattles overhead. A drink cart goes clattering down the aisle. The nose of the plane tips downward severely.

"But I haven't seen anything yet," I tell Cicely.

"I know," she says, her lips curling into a small smile.

I wake up in my king-sized bed, my arms tangled in moist sheets. I am still yelling *"No!!!"*—my heart pounding, my T-shirt soaked in sweat—when I sit bolt upright. The flat screen television is on. A woman is modeling cheap-looking jewelry on the Shopping Channel. Bowie is nowhere in sight. I wipe the sweat from my eyes and forehead with the back of my hand. I locate the remote beside a pillow, click the TV off, and fall back onto the mattress.

"Jesus," I say and lie there for awhile, shaking and trying to breathe as if I am calm.

But I'm not. My head is throbbing. It feels like someone has jammed a screwdriver in my right ear and is twisting, slowly, cruelly. I sit up again, massaging my temples, and reach over to the bedside table for my Crazy Pills. I chomp down three. Next to my bed, on the floor, is a two litre bottle of Orange Gatorade, which I must have put there before passing out. I take a few swigs. Pop a Halls into my mouth. Stick the Vicks inhaler up my left nostril. Then fall back into bed. I close my eyes and sleep.

When I wake again, I feel somewhat better. My headache is gone, but I'm still shaky, anxious, extremely tired. According to the digital clock on my dresser, it's 4:18 P.M. The blinds let in a little sunlight. It doesn't matter—the day's a write-off.

I get up and go to the washroom. Chew up three more pills and wash down their powdery residue with some cold tap water. I've now taken two more pills than I am supposed to take in a day, but I don't care. I need them now.

Back in my bedroom, I switch the ringer off on the phone and put a movie in the DVD player—*The Hunt For Red October*, it helps me sleep—then crawl back into bed. I finish off the Gatorade. Bowie jumps up on the bed, meows, then starts plucking himself a spot on the comforter near my hip. He lies down. I pet him absently. His fur is amazingly soft. I'm happy for the company.

I try not to think about anything. Clear my mind of all thought. I'm so drowsy, it works. I close my eyes again and slide into a long, drug-induced, dreamless sleep.

Book Three

Try Whistling This

For our first date, we meet up at a laundromat. I hate laundromats, but this one's actually cool. Not only do they have washing machines that hold up to sixty pounds of laundry and equally massive dryers, but they have a cozy little lounge area—away from the loud, scary machines—with a licensed snack bar, comfortable couches and arm chairs, a CD jukebox, a small library of fairly hip books, and a billiard table. I even like the name: Sips 'N' Suds.

"Sorry about the change of plans," Kathleen says.

"No worries," I say.

"My washer is on the fritz again and laundry was piled up to the ceiling. Literally."

"It's okay," I tell her. "I like this place. It's charming. Plus, they serve beer." I hold up my bottle of Canadian as proof. "Albeit domestic."

Kathleen smiles. It is beatific, her smile.

"Cheers," she says, holding up her Blue Light.

"Cheers."

We clink bottles and drink. It's a Monday afternoon. The only other person doing laundry is a gangly guy in his twenties. He's sitting on top of a folding table with headphones on, reading a chewed-up paperback. He looks content.

"You must be hungry," Kathleen says. "The sandwiches here are great, if you want something to tide you over."

"Oh, no. I'm fine, thanks," I say. "I rarely eat anyway. Well, I mean, I never eat breakfast and I often skip lunch. Usually I eat dinner when my stomach starts to growl or I feel lightheaded."

"Really? Breakfast is my favourite meal. In fact, my favourite food is bacon. Also, Ben & Jerry's ice cream. Also, chocolate mint fudge."

"Eeew. I hate fudge," I say then regret it. So I add, "Well, I dislike it, I mean. It's not my sworn enemy."

"Wow," Kathleen says. "How can anyone hate fudge?"

"It's just so ... sugary. Maybe I'd like it if I tried it again," I say.

"Maybe."

"I'm just not big on sweets."

"Oh, *I am*. I have the biggest sweet tooth in the *world*," Kathleen says. "I couldn't live without Ben & Jerry's ice cream. Seriously. It's like oxygen to me. And every summer I take Jonah to the Perth Fair and we load up at the Fudge Hut. They have the world's best fudge. We buy enough to practically fill a deep freezer. But listen to me," she says. "I sound like a junkie."

"But in a good way," I say, and she laughs.

When she laughs, I've noticed, she blinks her eyes. Her laugh is gentle and genuine, and puts me at ease. She rarely looks away from me. I keep looking at my Fender sneakers, like they're the world's most intriguing shoes. Although Kathleen's shoes might fit that bill: gold beaded Birkenstocks with tiny red hearts on the straps. They're adorable. They match her breezy outfit: broken in jeans, white T-shirt, funky plaid jacket and a flowered scarf. I'm no fashionista (I am, after all, wearing a graphic T-shirt that reads: "When you get sad, stop being sad and be awesome instead"—I mean, *come on!*), but it's clear Kathleen is in touch with her inner gypsy.

"You should model bohemian clothes," I tell her.

She looks down at her jacket. "Model? I'd fall flat on my face."

"No, not uppity high-end fashion with women in stiletto

heels and bird cages on their heads. Just cool, earthy, beatnik stuff," I say.

"Are you saying I look like a bag lady?"

"Oh my. God, no. I think you look amazing. Natural. Beautiful."

She blushes.

I drink some beer.

"You're very open and honest," she says.

I roll my eyes. "You have no idea," I say.

One of the industrial-sized machines makes an annoying buzzer-like noise.

"Fries are up," I say.

Kathleen laughs.

We get up and I help her fold her laundry.

~~~~~~

"I was at the video store the other night," Kathleen says, "and I go up to the counter and this bubbly little girl with glittering silver braces says to me, 'Did you find everything you were looking for, Ma'am?' And I just stood there thinking: She just called me 'Ma'am.' Did she seriously just call me 'Ma'am?' I mean, this girl was so young she likely doesn't know how to spell mortgage, but still. I thought, *Do I really look that old? Or is she just being polite?* Anyway, after I pay and everything I drive straight over to my mother's house and ring the doorbell. When she answered, I said, 'Mom, do I look old to you? Do I look thirty-three?' 'What are you doing here?' she says, all confused. 'Do you need me to baby-sit?' But I was serious. I was almost crying. I said, 'Mom, please just answer the question. Do I look
~~~~~~

old to you? Do I look thirty-three?' And my mom's kind of a jokey lady, so she says, 'You look *forty-three*. Do you want some vegetarian chili?' So I said, 'Be serious. I'm being serious.' And she said, 'Well, I don't know, sweetie. What does thirty-three really look like?' She said, 'I mean, what are you supposed to look like when you're thirty-three?' And I said, 'Exactly! Thank you, Mom. Thank you very much.' Then I drove straight home, put on *The Breakfast Club* and drank three-quarters of a bottle of red wine."

I laugh and rake a hand through my hair. "That's hilarious. Good choice with *The Breakfast Club*, too," I say.

"It's one of my favourite movies," she says. "I remember seeing it in the theater with Billy Davis when I was sixteen. I watch it at least once a year. I have to, it seems. Though I usually watch it with a bunch of girlfriends."

"Few people realize this," I say, "but Simple Minds did not write 'Don't You (Forget About Me).'"

"Hmm."

"Actually, forget I said that."

"What? Why?"

"I'm just full of useless trivia like that," I say. "Once I get started, it's hard to stop."

This is true. Especially about music. But movies, too. And books.

Kathleen laughs and cradles her pint of Carlsberg with both hands.

We're at Fitzgerald's now, having folded Kathleen's laundry, tucked it neatly into the back of her Subaru Forester, and driven the five blocks down Princess Street to get here. I was impressed by Kathleen's parallel parking prowess. Took her less than fifteen seconds to maneuver into a really tricky spot outside Sarah's Fine Foods.

"Wow," I'd said. "That was well done."

"I know," she'd said, smiling proudly. "It just comes naturally to me. I don't know why."

Now she's looking through a menu. Or, rather, she was. It's open on the table in front of her but now she's focused on me. She says, "I totally see my mother's point, though. You know? Who says what you're supposed to look like at any age? Or feel like, for that matter."

"I agree," I say. "I don't really give it any thought until my birthday rolls around."

"Oh God, *birthdays*," Kathleen says. "I nearly had a nervous breakdown when I turned thirty. And my friends threw me this giant surprise party, too. What a nightmare."

"I know what you mean. My thirty-second birthday was rough," I say. "My mom died when she was thirty-two."

I take a sip of Keith's. Kathleen's looking at me sympathetically, like my dog just died. "I'm so sorry," she says. "That's really sad."

I nod. "That's okay. Thank you. It was a long time ago."

"Well, yes, but that must have been really hard on you."

I clear my throat. "It was. I was only ten. My sister was twelve."

"What was she like—your mother?" Kathleen says.

"Well ...." I don't usually talk about this, about my mother, so I'm caught off guard. Takes me awhile to gather my thoughts. "She was shy and soft-spoken," I say. "Um. She was a photographer. So she worked out of her studio, at home. I don't think she had many friends; I mean, she wasn't a very social sort of person. She used to read to me all the time, random words from the dictionary. She was very sweet and patient. And quite pretty."

My voice trails off. I'm looking down at a coaster. I feel

orphaned, all over again. It's this hollow feeling I get, from time to time. Like I am completely alone on this planet. It depresses me, this feeling, but it only lasts about five minutes. Then I shake my head and force myself to think about something else. I try my best to do that now. I smile at Kathleen, and she smiles back and touches my hand. I'm tempted to reach out and touch her hair. Push her bangs back like she does.

Then Charlie, tonight's waiter, is upon us. His name's not really Charlie but I call him that (as do many other regulars) because he's nearly bald and often wears a T-shirt like Charlie Brown's: yellow with a black zigzag near the bottom. He's wearing it now.

"How's it goin', Finny? You folks ready to order?" he asks.

"I'm good for now, thanks." I dislike eating when I'm having a pint. "I might get something to munch on in a bit."

"Well, I'm starving," Kathleen says, scanning the menu. She clucks her tongue, smacks her lips. Then she folds up the menu and hands it to Charlie. "I'll have the pub wrap with the chef's salad instead of French fries."

"Dressing?"

"Oh. Ranch, please. On the side."

"Another Keith's, Finny?"

"Please," I say, and Charlie's off, leaving the acrid scent of Polo cologne behind him. It's like an invisible cloud that slowly passes.

When he's definitely out of ear shot, Kathleen leans closer to me and says, "Does that guy remind you of Charlie Brown?"

"A little," I tell her.

~~~~~~
~~~~~~

It's a great date. We talk and laugh a lot. I order a small plate of nachos and Kathleen helps me eat them before the cheese congeals. She nearly keeps up with me, too, pint for pint. And she apologizes when she says she has to call her baby-sitter. How sweet is that?

There is no doubt: I am absolutely falling in love with this woman.

"Suzie," she says. Suzie is a friend and a colleague, Kathleen's told me, a grown woman not a bubble gum-chomping teenager. They work together in the Intensive Care Unit at Kingston Mercy. "I don't think I'll be able to drive home. I'm a little tipsy," Kathleen says. Her cell phone is black, sleek, no-nonsense. "So I can just leave the car here and take a taxi home later on. Although I do have three baskets of laundry in the trunk. How's Jonah?"

Jonah is her ten-year-old son. I learned this during the two-hour phone conversation we had when I called to ask her out. Also, she's divorced. Been divorced for eight years. Her ex-husband's name is Ted. He runs a landscaping business. Long story short: he was jealous and, once, physically abusive. He was so insecure and jealous, at one point, he would follow Kathleen to work because he didn't believe she was working. Can you imagine that? Being trailed to work by your mate? Things got worse. He said he wondered if Jonah was really his son. He kept close tabs on Kathleen's credit card bills and their joint bank accounts. He hunted through her purse looking for motel receipts or something similarly incriminating. Then one day, for no good reason at all, he slammed Kathleen up against a wall. And that was that. The next day she made an appointment with a lawyer and began the process of filing for divorce.

I love it that she was so resolute. So decisive. No one was going to push her around. Nor will they ever, for that matter, it's clear; at least it's clear to me. Kathleen has a steely determination, which I admire and find fascinating and sexy.

Suzie tells her Jonah's fine. (I can hear her voice, loud and clear.) They were just playing Monopoly and eating popcorn, she says. Then Suzie offers to swing by and pick up Kathleen's laundry.

"No, that's okay, Suze. But thanks," Kathleen says. She covers the phone with one hand and whispers to me, "She just wants to meet you," she tells me, and I laugh.

This is definitely going places, I can feel it. And not just because one of her friends wants to meet me. It's more than that. Kathleen is so naturally happy and funny and sweet, it excites me. It excites me that I'm with her; it excites me that she wants to be here with me. Also, she's forthright and genuine, a free spirit who talks as much as I do, which I like because she's not much for small talk. She pretty much cuts to the meaty parts, the stuff in life that truly matters. And when I talk, she really listens and cares. She's kind and thoughtful and open-minded.

Do I mind that she has a son? Not at all. I have two nephews around the same age as Jonah, and ten's a good age, I think. You can talk like an adult to a ten-year-old, and they're often smarter than you think. And I don't believe in all that stuff about "baggage." To me, it's ridiculous. We all have *baggage*, if you want to call it that (I don't; I hate the term), because we've all lived and experienced things. The fact that Kathleen has a son intrigues me. She's obviously experienced different aspects of life than I have: giving birth, raising a child—which are as foreign to me as Euclidean geometry or building a rocket ship.

Screw *baggage*.

Also, I'm assured the ex-husband is completely out of the

picture. Which, more than anything, makes me happy and relieved for Kathleen and her son. The guy sounds like a first-class jerk. It's good for Kathleen and Jonah he's not around. Otherwise, it wouldn't matter much to me.

It's like Kathleen is reading my mind, too.

When I get back from using the washroom, she says to me, "It was a mistake, really, marrying Ted. But I was young. And he really had me fooled. He did. He seemed like a very sweet guy when we first got together. And not to make excuses for him, but I think he changed a lot after Jonah was born. Which really isn't an excuse—but I'm not sure he was ready to settle down just yet. Still. Where his jealousy came from, I've no idea. But I wasn't going to put up with it. I guess I did for six months or so, but even then it didn't feel right to me ... I felt sick to my stomach every time I grabbed my purse and noticed everything was out of place. And when he started following me to work, then I got really scared. But I was afraid if I did or said anything, he might snap. It was like he'd turned into a whole different person. Certainly not the person I'd married and certainly not anyone I wanted to be around. Then when he threw me against that wall, well ... that was it. It was almost a relief, really. I woke Jonah up, scooped him out of bed, and took him to my mother's. It was like a giant weight had been lifted; I could feel it in the pit of my stomach. Or rather, I *couldn't* feel it anymore—that horrible feeling of uneasiness, of being on edge. It disappeared."

All I can say to that is, "Wow. I can only imagine," and then, "Good for you."

She gulps down a mouthful of beer, then says, "Okay. New subject. Tell me about your writing. I've never met a published author before."

"Blah. I don't know," I say. But then Kathleen makes this

scrunched-up face, like's she cranky, and starts groaning. "Okay, okay." I laugh. "Stop that."

She stops. I laugh again. There's a Guinness clock above the bar, and I look over at it. "No! Don't tell me the time," Kathleen says, giggling, covering her eyes. "I'm having too much fun. I don't want to know. Talk or I'll start groaning again."

I love that she's this silly. You must need to possess this sort of temperament to work in Intensive Care and remain sane, at day's end. Maybe I'll bring that up later.

"Well, let me see," I say. "I've written three books. Two novels and a children's book. The children's book is called *The Water Bear*, it's based on a story my grandfather used to tell me. My friend Fiona did the illustrations."

"What's it about?"

"Basically, it's about a bear that eats children."

"A *children's* book?"

"Well, it's a cautionary tale. Let me finish."

"Okay, okay. You go."

I go.

"My Gramps had this huge lower backyard at his house in North Bay, and there was a series of huge pine trees at the end of it and, beyond those, a stream. Gramps was always afraid one of us—me or my sister or one of my cousins—would be playing down there and slip on a rock or something and somehow end up drowning. So he made up this story. He told us there was a huge water bear that lived down there and would eat any child who happened to pass beyond the pine trees. And the story stuck with me because it scared the hell out of me when I was a boy. 'Can it open doors?' I'd ask him. 'Can it chew through glass? Can it climb stairs?' And he'd laugh his hearty laugh and say, 'No, the water bear only eats children who wander into its territory, beyond the pine trees.' He was a great storyteller," I say.

"Sounds like it," Kathleen says.

"I'll have to get you a copy," I tell her.

"I'd like that. And what about your novels?"

"They don't sell very well," I say.

"Be serious. I'd like to hear."

"All right. Well, the first one I wrote is called *The Orphan Diaries*, and it's not very uplifting, I'm afraid. It's essentially the story of my childhood, and losing my parents at such a young age and being very fearful and such. I fictionalized it, though really it's autobiographical. It got some decent reviews. Anyway, it was cathartic to write.

"The second novel is much more lighthearted. Or at least I meant it to be. I took some flack from a couple of religious groups over it, but it also got some decent reviews. It's about three sisters who start a rock band called *The Virtues*—which is also the title of the book—and they become somewhat successful: have a couple of radio hits, make a few videos, tour North America and such. But they end up failing miserably in the end because, well ... they're all sort of basket cases."

"Uh-huh. How so?" Kathleen smiles, resting her chin in her palm, her elbow on the table. She's had four pints, I think. She looks quite relaxed, happy to be listening to me. And I think she's starting to get the idea that I could talk all night, and she'd be right. Because I could. Easily. And I'd love to but tonight that seems out of the question.

"Okay, well, there's Hope, the lead singer, who is an angry sort and chronically depressed; then there's Faith, the drummer, who is addicted to opium and thinks God is dead; and the third sister, the guitar player, is Chastity, who is incurably promiscuous and keeps sleeping with her sisters' boyfriends. So, you get the idea."

"Wow, that's fascinating. And funny," Kathleen says, and laughs. "Seriously. You've an incredibly vivid imagination. I could never dream up that kind of thing."

I sigh, shrug my shoulders, blush. I'm not very good at accepting compliments.

"No, really. I can't wait to read them."

"I think a couple of used book stores in town may have a copy," I tell her.

"Oh, stop it," she says. "You should be proud. Don't put yourself down like that."

I meet her eyes. She looks dead serious. "Okay," I say.

"I'm allowed to scold you, you know," she says.

"Why's that?"

"Because *you* asked *me* out."

And right now, as happy as I am, as carefree as I'm feeling, that makes complete and perfect sense.

~~~~~~

Tuesday afternoon, Fiona and I go grocery shopping. We go to the gargantuan Loblaws near our old high school because Fiona loves the huge produce section. She refuses to shop at any other grocery store. I push my cart around, not really knowing what I need but picking things off shelves here and there, sort of willy-nilly: a box of crackers, plum sauce, three different types of cereal, a case of Gatorade Mango Electrico. Basically, I follow Fiona, who is pokey and likes to read labels carefully and squeeze melons and the like.

"So how was the big date?" Fiona asks me in the produce section.
~~~~~~

Her tone is friendly enough, but I can tell she's upset because she used the word *big*. It's a telltale sign she's perturbed. I'm used to this from Fiona; she's been jealous of every girlfriend I've ever had, dating back to grade school and girls I kissed behind portables at recess.

"Fine," I tell her. "Good."

She's thoroughly inspecting tomatoes, holding them up to the light, twisting and turning them in her hand. Then she places the good ones in a plastic bag.

"Did you bring her home and bang her?" she asks, with only a little more venom in her tone.

"*Pardon?*"

"Did you charm her panties off?"

I shake my head. "Oh, come on, Fee," I say. "Don't be crude. It wasn't like that. It was different. *She* is different."

Placing the bag of tomatoes in her cart, Fiona considers this. Then she moves on to the cucumber bin.

"I'm being *crude?*" she says, not facing me. "Here's your history, Finny: You meet a woman for drinks, bring them back to your place, charm them, and then screw them silly. Oh, and in between you might have more drinks and let them choose what music they'd like to hear, then regale them with stories about how passionate a man Bono is and how Neil Finn is such an underrated songwriter. Sound familiar?"

It does. And I hate that she's right. But ... "So what?" I snap, raising my voice a little. "At least I'm genuine. I mean, I happen to *like* having people over to my place for drinks. And people seem to like to come over to my place. You make it sound like I force alcohol down their throats. And yes, I also happen to think that Neil Finn is a brilliant *and* hugely underrated songwriter. And again, *yes!*—I think Bono's a very passionate man and a great humanitarian. I admit all that. So what exactly is your point, Fee?"

Inspecting a cucumber, she looks unruffled, her chin held high. "My point is simple," she says. "When you have a date, you usually end up screwing your date."

"Please stop using that word," I tell her. A woman in an orange spring jacket, walking by with a basket in her hand, looks at us suspiciously out the corner of her eye.

"*Screwing?* That's suddenly obscene to you?" Fiona says with bitter sarcasm.

"It is if you're referring to Kathleen," I say.

"Aaah, I see."

"Fiona. What the hell is wrong with you? I walked Kathleen to the street so she could get a taxi. I had my hand on the small of her back, and when the cab came, I gave her a kiss. She smelled like vanilla and sunshine, and tasted like grapes. Is that what you want to hear? All the *gory* details?"

Now she starts to sulk. Frowning, she sets the cucumber she's been holding back on the pile of cucumbers, and pushes her cart hastily toward the bread section—one of the carts' wheels catching and squeaking annoyingly on the tile floor. After a moment, I follow her. She thumps open a Plexiglas lid, snatches a pair of tongs, and begins picking up and looking at sesame seed bagels. She rips a plastic bag off the giant roll, then can't seem to decide which bagels she wants. She sniffles. Looks to her left, hiding her face from me.

"Can you meet me in the frozen food section in ten minutes?" she asks, her voice wavering, lifting up then diving down, cracking in the middle.

I take in a deep breath. "Yeah."

I wheel my cart to the front of the store and momentarily abandon it by the turnstiles. But there's no way out. So I have to leap over a newspaper display case. I land sort of awkwardly, and the woman working the Express Aisle cash register gives me a strange, sideways look.

Outside, it's a wonderfully sunny day: the perfect mix of bright, warming sunshine and cool spring breeze. I light a Silk Cut and pace around.

One of these days, I think, Fiona will go too far. Say something not just over-the-top, because she's always saying things that are over-the-top, but something, I don't know ... so unthinkably hurtful, I won't be able to walk it off.

When we were both in university, Fiona played twice a week at the Red Leaf Tavern, a cheap, dingy place in the student ghetto. One night in the middle of her set, some boozed-up businessman began shouting at the bartender. "What the Christ is this?! I can piss colder than this!" he'd said, thumping his pint glass of beer on the bar, sloshing suds everywhere. And the bartender just sort of rolled his eyes and let it go; was ready to pour the guy another drink, but Fiona stopped playing. She sat there a few moments, glaring at the guy, then spoke into the microphone. "And what is *this?*" she'd said. "Lookit here, folks. This well-mannered gentleman claims he can piss cold beer! Well, isn't that just the cat's pajamas. Who here would like to see this gluttonous swillbowl piss a few pitchers of ice cold beer? Anyone?"

Once they caught on to what was happening, the small crowd began to laugh. Then a few people hollered for the guy to shut up or get out. Then a table of law students began throwing peanuts at him, pelting the guy, rapid-fire—*thwack! thwack! thwack!*—so that you could hear the peanuts rapping off his skull. Eventually, he was forced to leave with his suit coat over his head.

Another time, she'd broken up with some boyfriend or other (Bill? Phil? Will?) but, for months after, he kept drunk dialing her and coming by her apartment in the wee hours, standing in the street, and yelling up at Fiona's window. So one night, instead of calling the cops, she opened her window and poked her head out, a megaphone held up to her mouth. "Nobody cares what you're saying," she'd said, and the megaphone amplified her voice tenfold but also made earsplitting shrieking noises on its own. "You have a one inch penis. Go away!"

In the book shop one day, when Fiona was in a bad mood and a man was buying *The Da Vinci Code*, she'd told him he must be a complete idiot.

She's certainly not above saying hurtful things.

The thing is, I know she's jealous. And I know she's not naturally mean-spirited; that's just her way, sometimes. She says what she feels. She always has, and she likely always will.

I finish my smoke and head back into the grocery store, find my cart and wheel on back to the frozen foods. Fiona's at the end of the aisle, standing by her cart, reading the back of a Lean Cuisine box. Without looking up, she says, "I'm sorry."

"It's all right," I say.

We're quiet a moment. From hidden speakers high above comes the sound of Manfred Mann's Earth Band's version of "Blinded By The Light." I'd like to tell Fiona it's a Springsteen song, but she knows this bit of rock trivia, too, I'm fairly sure.

"Hmm. Two-hundred and forty calories," she says. "Only five grams of fat. And no preservatives." She looks up at me and says, "Not bad. Cheese Cannelloni. Want some?"

"Sure," I say. "Load me up."

And she does. Starts dumping them into my cart by the handful. We get to laughing. Then we count them up.

"Fifty-two," Fiona says.

"Really?" I say "I got fifty."

"You always did suck at math," she says.

~~~~~~

We're driving down Concession Street—Fiona's driving, actually, and I'm nervously tugging on my seat belt—when we nearly get sideswiped by a woman in a crappie old Datsun. Some blind or idiotic woman behind the wheel of an orange shit-heap from the '70s cuts us off, suddenly swerving into our lane.

I'm ticked off. But Fiona loses it. She lays on the horn, and says, "You bitch!"

"Easy," I say. This is my car, after all: a shiny red fairly new Mini Cooper. I know, I know: it may seem ridiculous that I own a car when I don't even have a driver's license. But here's my reasoning: first, I can afford it. (I can afford to buy a small fleet of Mini Coopers, actually, but that's beside the point.) Second, Fiona uses the car to take me where I want and I also sometimes let her use it to get to gigs. Plus, it's handy when I get the urge to head out on a sudden road trip to Toronto or Ottawa or my sister's cottage, wherever. Granted, on such occasions, I need to find someone who wants to go with me and is willing, and able, to drive my car. But that's not usually a problem. Fiona pays for gas, and I pay for insurance and parking. To me, it's a sweet deal.

But I don't want my sporty little car shredded by some ugly, oil-spitting relic.

"What an *unbelievable moron!* Can you believe that?" Fiona asks me. She steps on the accelerator and we lurch forward.

"Whoa, Fee, take it easy," I say.

But she speeds up even more, checks the rearview mirror, then quickly switches lanes. We pull up beside the woman in the
~~~~~~

Datsun. She's chomping on a wad of gum and wearing huge, square sunglasses and a Nike visor. I dislike her even more now. Fiona hits the button and puts her window down. She holds up her middle finger, stiffly. Her cheeks are really red, like apples about to burst.

"Hey lady!" she yells, and the lady looks over. "This is my middle finger," Fiona screams at her. "So ... So ... So *fucking look at it!!!*"

The woman's jaw drops. She seems to shrink into her seat. Then she falls behind, likely in shock, and Fiona speeds up a little.

I don't say a word, not wanting to inflame the situation.

A few blocks on, Fiona lets out a massive sigh. Some normal colouring returns to her face. She breathes in some cool air then puts her window back up.

"Oh my God, that felt good," she says, an intoxicated, crazed look in her eyes like she's just ridden the greatest, loopiest roller coaster on earth. "Wanna hit the highway?" she says.

"No, thank you," I say. "Home'd be good."

<div align="center">~~~~~~</div>

"You remember that guy I was telling you about?" Fiona says.

"The stalker guy?"

"No."

"Guy with the lamb chop sideburns?

"No-*oh*," she says, irritated. "Layton. Cute bartender at The Duck and Dog. Saving up to open his own place. Always tanned from sailing."

"Doesn't ring a bell, Fee."

She's helping me put away my groceries. Not that I need the help. Nor did I ask for it. Fiona volunteered. Actually, she just sort of followed me upstairs. Truth be told, she's being rather clingy. After her little outburst at the grocery store, I feel like some alone time. Some Fiona-less time.

"Well, he's been asking me out for ages," she tells me. "And I thought I'd finally say yes."

She's posturing. There's no doubt in my mind. And I'm not really in the mood for it.

"Well, that's good," I tell her. I take a bag of Cool Ranch Doritos out of one of the cardboard boxes holding my groceries, and Bowie trots over and rubs up against my leg, meowing, tail hooked in the air. I put the bag in a cupboard, then kneel down to pet him. "Who wants a Bowie treat?" I ask him, and he answers with a louder meow. It's hard to believe he's fifteen. Although I don't like to think about that. I wipe some sleep from one of his eyes, rub his ears. He begins to purr loudly. "Handsome man," I tell him.

"It's great," Fiona says. "He's a wonderful guy. He's not a poseur, you know. I mean, he goes to the gym but he doesn't brag about it; you can just tell. And he's not just out to get laid, either, even though he's beautiful and could get any woman he wanted. I like it that he's sort of shy. Well, not shy exactly. But he listens to you and you know he cares, and he's not always trying to one up you or talk over you. He's very unassuming."

I yawn. "Well ... good."

Fiona nods, opening a bag of Oreo cookies, which I'd specifically bought with Kathleen in mind. "I'll let him ask me out again but this time I'll say yes. I play at The Duck on Friday," she tells me.

I'm about to yawn again. I try not to, but I do anyhow. "That's great," I say. Then: "Fee, I don't mean to be rude, but I could really use a nap. I'm bag tired."

She's eating a cookie. "Oh. Okay, then." She sets the open bag of Oreos on the kitchen counter. "Do you mind if I take the car for the afternoon? I need to run a few more errands."

"No, not at all."

When she leaves, I put all the frozen food in the freezer, tuck the milk in the refrigerator and leave the rest. I toss my jean jacket over a kitchen chair, shuck off my sneakers and leave them on the floor by Bowie's food and water bowls. Then I head into the living room, turn on a fan for white noise, curl up on the most comfortable couch I own with a cashmere throw and quickly fall asleep.

~~~~~~

I'm at Kathleen's house for dinner, and I'm really nervous. I brought six bottles of Heineken, a bottle of red wine—something called Yellow Tail, which Kathleen said she liked (I know nothing about wine)—a signed copy of *The Water Bear*, and a modest bouquet of spring flowers: lilies, tulips, daffodils, daisies, magnolias. But I'm beginning to think I should have brought more booze.

Kathleen looks beautiful in a simple light blue baby doll dress with the tiniest shoulder straps I've ever seen. *Isn't she afraid they'll snap?* I wonder. They're as thin as pencils. But she doesn't seem concerned. She flies around the kitchen, talking to me while opening the oven and inspecting the chicken; then she checks the rice cooker; then pours herself a glass of wine. And finally she arranges the bouquet of flowers just so in a glass vase in the centre of the table.

I'm sitting at the table drinking a beer. "You're making me dizzy," I tell her. "Do you need any help?"
~~~~~~

"No, I'm fine. Thanks. It's just—" She looks around, biting her lower lip. The kitchen is white and blue, with stainless steel appliances, a big island with a double sink, glassed-in cupboards I recognize from the Ikea catalogue, and a charming antique table with legs thick as tree stumps. I think it's oak—it's golden brown, like a digestive cookie—but I definitely could be wrong about that. "Where did I put my glass of wine?" Kathleen says, almost to herself.

"On the island," I tell her.

"Oh. Thank you." She sits down on a stool at the island, lifts her glass, and takes a sip. "Yummy," she says.

"You know, I'm beginning to like your schedule," I say. "Four days on, three days off. Three days on, four days off. It must feel like you're getting a mini-vacation every couple of days."

"Sort of. But switching from days to nights is a pain," she says. "I need to sleep during the day sometimes and adjust my system so that I'm wide awake and ready to go at eleven at night. It can be draining. Takes some time to get used to. And sometimes it feels like I only see Jonah in passing for days at a time. He'll be at school, I'll be at work. Then I'll pick him up from the baby-sitter's and he's fast asleep. We'll rent a movie and I'm snoring away five minutes into it."

I think that's what I'm nervous about, actually: meeting Jonah *with* his mother. I mean, obviously they know one another quite well, which gives me an outsider sort of feeling. Like they might gang up on me or something.

But that doesn't happen.

Turns out Jonah is a delightful little lad. He has the same sunny, easygoing demeanor as his mother. They look quite a bit alike, too: Jonah has the same bright brown eyes and pale skin as Kathleen, and he's been allowed to grow his hair a bit shaggy for a ten-year-old, but it has the same rich texture and chestnut colouring as Kathleen's.

He was playing at a friend's house, it turns out. First thing he says to me when he walks in the door is: "Hello, Finny. I'm Jonah. It's nice to meet you." Then he shakes my hand, formally, firmly, although my hand could swallow two of his. He comes off as a confident little adult. I shoot Kathleen a look but she's smiling absently at her son.

"Well, hey, Jonah. I'm Finny," I say. "It's nice to meet you."

"So you're a writer?" he says.

"I am."

"You write novels?"

"I have, yes."

"You make lots of money?"

"I *have* lots of money," I say, laughing, "but not from writing books."

"Oh," he says. "Well, that's okay, too. So you write because you like to?"

"Exactly."

Then Kathleen says, "Jonah, is that the shirt you were wearing earlier?"

He's wearing baggy jeans, well-worn Chuck Taylors, a white polo shirt, and a scruffy corduroy jacket. The polo shirt does look out of place; it is blindingly white and looks new. Everything else Jonah's wearing might have come from a thrift shop.

"No," he says. "My shirt got dirty when I was playing goalie, so Milton's mother made me change into one of his."

"Is it dirty or is it *wrecked?*" Kathleen asks him.

He smiles, half playful, half sorry. "Maybe wrecked. But I was playing goalie, Mom. I was diving all over the road."

"Milton's mom let you play on the road?"

"Well, not really. Mostly in the driveway."

"Okay, I don't want to think about it right now," Kathleen says. "I'll talk to her later on. You go wash up before dinner, please."

"Yes, Mom."

She takes his face in her hands and kisses him on top of the head. Then he runs out of the room, down a hallway, and noisily up a flight of stairs. *Thump-tha-thump, thump-tha-thump, thump-tha-thump.*

I open a second beer as Kathleen prepares the chicken. She won't even let me watch. "It's a secret recipe," she tells me. "Sit down. Relax. Enjoy your beer."

"I smell curry," I say.

"Oh, hush."

Finally, I get to do something: set the table. Fresh from cleaning up, Jonah helps me, which I'm grateful for because all I know to do is to put a fork on the left side of a plate and a knife on the other. Jonah works out the kinks, adjusting my handiwork here and there, and neatly setting down cloth napkins and salad forks and tiny spoons, until it all looks very tidy.

Then, just as we're about to eat, my cell phone rings. "I'm sorry," I tell Kathleen. "I'll just let it go to voicemail."

"Well, no," she says. "What if it's important?"

I can't imagine anyone phoning me for something important, I'd like to tell her. Instead, I nod and say, "Maybe you're right." I grab the phone from the inside pocket of my suit coat. It's Julia's cellphone number.

"Hi, Jules."

"I've been b-b-b-burgled," she says. She's crying.

"*Burgled?* You mean, robbed? Mugged? What?"

"I mean ...." There's a pause, but not a silent one: Julia's gasping for air, making quiet whimpering noises.

"Are you okay, Jules?"

"I was *burgled!*" she cries. "Robbed. Someone b-b-b-b-broke into my apartment. Sh-sh-sh-shimmied the lock or something ...."

"*Jimmied* the lock? Were you home? Where are you?"

I shouldn't be asking so many questions. Julia will just get more upset and find it harder to speak. And I feel like an idiot blathering away at the table, with Kathleen and Jonah looking at me strangely, so I excuse myself and wander into the dining room.

"I'm home now," she says. "But I'm really upset and I didn't know who else to c-c-c-call. The police said I should get a new lock for my door and so ...."

While I'm waiting for Jules to heave up her next words, I check out the dining room. Nice beige area rug. An old, repainted hutch, the colour of coffee with milk. Some framed photos of Kathleen and Jonah hang on one wall, as well as a few of a handsome older couple I assume are Kathleen's parents.

Julia sighs. "And so I'm waiting for the locksmith, but he's late."

"Where's Nighthawk?"

I feel ridiculous even saying the name. Nighthawk is Julia's neighbour. She's a lesbian sculptor who works at an AIDS hospice. I only put it that way because when I met her, she shook my hand and said, "I'm Nighthawk, a lesbian sculptor who works at an AIDS hospice." And she seemed quite comfortable saying it.

"I don't know. She's not in," Julia says. "But I don't want to wait alone."

"So, were you home when this happened?"

"No. But they stole all my jewelry, my laptop, my iPod, and eight hundred dollars."

"*Eight hundred dollars?* In cash?"

"*Yes!* I know. It's fucking ... s-s-s-stupid. But I just took it out yesterday to pay my parents back some money they loaned me. I only had the ... m-m-m-money one day. I hid it in my laptop bag."

Her crying is louder now. It's more like wailing. I feel horrible for her. That is some seriously lousy luck! I tell her I'll be over in ten minutes.

"That sounded bad," Kathleen says. "Is everything okay?"

"No, my friend Julia's been robbed and she's freaking out," I say. "I'm sorry, but I really have to go."

"Oh my God, I'm so sorry."

"I need to call a cab," I say. Then I realize I have a phone in my hand. I key in the numbers for Harley's Taxi, which I know by heart. "She only needs someone to stay with her for a little while," I tell Kathleen. "Until the locksmith gets there. So I can come back a bit later."

"Yes. Okay. I hope she's all right," Kathleen says.

A man with a gruff, guttural voice answers the phone. I tell him I need a cab ... then I look helplessly at Kathleen, mouth open.

"228 Nelson Street," she whispers.

"At 228 Nelson Street," I tell the dispatcher. "Going uptown. Thanks."

The next few minutes are kind of awkward. I apologize about ten times, then say "shit" twice and apologize again for that, both times. I tell Jonah it was nice meeting him, and maybe I'll see him later. He says it was nice meeting me, too. Kathleen gets up, though I plead with her not to. "Please, no. You made a delicious looking meal," I say. "Enjoy it. I'm so sorry." Then the taxi arrives and the cabbie honks the horn, and Kathleen comes over to where I'm standing by the door and gives me a quick kiss on the cheek. And I feel all flustered, I don't know what to say. So I just sort of wave my hands in the air, gesturing that sometimes life is just screwy. And Kathleen nods and smiles, as if to say: *I know.* "I'll be back soon, I hope," I tell her. Then I hurry down the driveway and jump in the back seat of the taxi.

~~~~~~

When I get there Julia's sitting on her front porch, smoking a joint. I sit down beside her. She's wearing a navy blue track suit and extremely white running shoes. Her shoulders are hunched, her dirty blonde hair in a loose ponytail. She lives on a pleasant, tree-lined street, with small clapboard houses jumbled close to one another, yellow lights glowing in their curtained windows. A white-haired man across the street sitting in a lawn chair on his front stoop, plays guitar and sings a Neil Young song— "Harvest Moon." He has a wonderful singing voice, low and melodic. If I had a harmonica on me, I'd be tempted to join him.

"Nice night," Julia says.

"Yes, it is."

Two boys speed by on fancy bicycles.

"Last one home's a pickled egg," one of them says.

"It's rotten egg, you dolt," says the other.

Julia chuckles. We watch them veer off around a corner. Their voices fade away.

Julia says, "They stole my grandmother's wedding ring." She takes a drag off her joint. The pot smells like some exotic coffee. She waits a moment, then exhales.
~~~~~~

"Oh no. I'm sorry, Jules," I say.

"I don't have the heart to tell my mother."

"Right."

It's a clear night. Just a sliver of a moon. A few visible stars. The old man finishes with "Harvest Moon," then starts strumming another song which I don't recognize. He hums the melody.

"All my life," Julia says, "I've been trying to figure out why bad things happen to good people. Is it all just random?"

I think about my parents. I can't remember the last thing I said to my father, but it wasn't nice. We were arguing. I was a stupid teenager saying stupid things. "I haven't the faintest idea, Jules," I say.

"All I want is a ten-minute conversation with God," she says. "That's all I'd need: ten minutes."

It hits me: Julia doesn't stutter when she's stoned.

I light a cigarette. Blow smoke rings above my head, watch them expand then break up and disappear. "Assuming there is a God," I say.

All *my* life, I've wondered if God exists. And I've believed He or She does exist, and my thinking's been basic: I *am* here, on Earth, and someone made me; and someone or some *thing* made the Earth. To me, it seemed impossible to imagine anything else.

Like I said, my thinking's been basic. And maybe even flawed. (I know little about the Big Bang theory, and thinking about it can send me into a panic, so I've never read about it.) But I pray, all the time. I pray for a clean, close shave. I pray for quick, panic-free showers. I pray Fiona will be happier. I pray that God will bless my sister and her boys and me, and that we'll all live long, healthy, happy, and quality lives. I pray my parents are together in Heaven. And happy. And that they didn't feel much pain when they died. Sometimes it feels like I'm begging instead of praying. For panic to go away. For God to quell my fears, to rid me of anxiety and shoot it off harmlessly into space.

I pray that Kathleen is the woman that will truly fall in love with me, and *stay* with me.

Julia and I wait for the locksmith.

~~~~~~~

I've been seeing Doc Marten for five years now. Here, in no particular order, is a short list of the things the Doc and I have established I'm afraid of: thunderstorms, death, driving, flying, fear itself, dental work, roller coasters, infinity, bossy strangers, bridges, mice, heights, snakes, insects, old age, responsibility, change, and being buried alive, a fear which Doc Marten finds particularly irrational.

"Some people *aren't* afraid of being buried alive?" I once asked him.

"It's really not likely to happen, so it doesn't enter into most people's everyday thoughts," was his measured response.

"Well, it seems like a rational fear to me," I'd told him. "I'd think you'd actually have to be rather *irrational* not to fear being buried alive." Then I'd asked him, "Do you fear it?"

"Not really," he'd said, which was an unusually vague answer, I'd thought. Then he'd added: "It's called taphephobia."

I'm in his office today. His name is not really Doc Marten, of course; it's Doctor Graham. But I've been calling him Doc Marten for years now because of the trendy boots he is fond of wearing. He's in his early forties. He's boyishly handsome with
~~~~~~~

shiny hair so blonde it sometimes appears yellow, and he wears stylish button-down shirts and expensive designer pants. It's like he's just walked off the pages of a glossy J. Crew magazine ad. Smart, studious and serious-minded, he is sort of dull, but he often helps me sort out my messed-up life, so I enjoy our visits.

Today we're talking about relationships. I've told him all about Kathleen and how wonderful I think she is, but I've made it clear I don't want to screw up this time.

"Do you think it's you who's been 'screwing up' in the past?" he asks me.

Oh, the question game! How fun, I think. "Well, it's been made quite clear to me in the past," I say, "by various people, that yes, it's been me who's screwed up. Acted like a frightened boy. Drank too much. Insulated myself with possessions."

"But what do *you* think?" he asks me.

"I think, if I could go back ... I might do some things differently," I say. "So that's a yes, I guess."

"You'd like to change some of your behaviours, then?"

"If that will help, yes."

"Do *you* think it will help?"

"I don't think it would hurt," I say, and Doc Marten smiles.

"I agree," he says.

We're both sitting in comfortable leather chairs, surrounded by shelves filled with thick, musty-smelling books, a leather ottoman separating us. A tall window in one corner lets in just a slice of sunlight, the brown curtains left open a crack. And five floors below, there's a lovely view of Kingston's waterfront. Although it's not lovely for me. I have to trick myself into thinking we're on the second or third floor to avoid having a panic attack. I like that my chair is facing Doc Marten and not the window.

Quite seriously, I say, "I truly think I'm in love with this woman. I know we've only been on three or four dates, but we've talked a lot—hours and hours and hours on the phone, too—and everything just *feels* right. We're on the same wave length. She gets me. I get her. And her son, Jonah, is a cute, funny, brilliant little boy who makes me feel ... I don't know ... like an adult. Because he cares about what I say. He looks up to me. I feel like he's making me ... a better person. More mature. And Kathleen, too—although we laugh a lot and fool around and act silly. I feel more mature around her, as well."

"It sounds like she and her son have really had quite a positive effect on you," Doc Marten says. "You seem much happier than when we last spoke. More self-assured. Less anxious."

"I am," I say, making a sweeping gesture with my arms, like: *who knew?* I'm smiling. Tapping my feet. "I'm really, truly happy. Although I'm worried ...."

Doc Marten's smiling, too, but I sense he's being cautious as well. His arms are folded across his lap. He seems too relaxed. "Worried about ...?"

"Fiona. She's really jealous," I say. "She's been dropping by all the time, calling me more than usual. I know her. She's acting odd. She's been doing this for decades, though. I shouldn't be surprised, I guess. But she's, well, an *extreme* sort of person. I think she's even been faking going on dates. To make me jealous, I mean. I'm just worried about her, is all."

"You're worried about what she'll do?"

"Yes," I say, then pause a moment for thought. The thoughts and words are in my head but I need to sort them out first, align them correctly. I breathe in deeply, then exhale. "Okay. The thing is, I think this might be a lasting relationship. And I'm thirty-two. I might be ready to settle down. And well, I'm just not sure Fiona would be prepared to deal with that ... very well."

Doc Marten nods, considering this. "You can't control her actions."

"No."

"You also can't control her emotions."

"No."

"I think it would be best for you to be perfectly honest with her. Be truthful in a gentle manner," Doc Marten says.

Be truthful in a gentle manner. I repeat the sentence in my head. I like it. *Maybe it's time to be more truthful with myself, too?* I think. Although I believe I'm getting there.

"I like the sound of that," I tell Doc Marten.

When our session ends, he refills my prescriptions, gives me a chummy pat on the arm, and says goodbye. I leave his office feeling like I've won a battle. A knot in my stomach has been untangled, it feels like. I walk down the hallway with a confident strut, sighing again and again, but with relief not anxiety. Outside the hospital, I fill my lungs with cool spring air, grateful for the sunlight warming my face, and I hit the sidewalk feeling light and airy and wonderfully content: a man who knows where he is going.

~~~~~~

I'm up early, watching the sunrise out my kitchen window. Birds are chirping. Looks like the sky is blushing. A man and woman, in exercise wear and sweaters, walk quickly through the courtyard. Well, they sort of waddle. They're speed walking.

It's 5:55 A.M. I make a wish. I wish for normalcy. A more normal life, that's what I wish for. So I eat breakfast. That seems a good place to start. I have a toasted bagel smothered with peanut butter and a tall, cold glass of milk. It tastes delicious.
~~~~~~

I have no plans for the day, but I get dressed and think about doing something I've wanted to do for years now: volunteer at a mental health crisis centre. I used to call their telephone hotline all the time, but haven't in years—haven't needed to. I've been able to cope with my panic attacks on my own. Reasonably well, anyway. I could easily help someone else do the same, I believe. Talk them down, so to speak, from that fearful tightrope. That would feel good, helping someone like me. I wonder if I'll have to take a training course.

Bowie follows me around the apartment, meowing. "Mornin', little man," I tell him. Then I refill his water bowl and freshen up his food. He eats with his eyes shut. This morning, watching him eat almost makes me cry. Cats are brilliant friends. Bending down to give him a good chin scratching, I notice that he has threads of grey in his coat. His nose is cold and wet. He's purring like crazy. "I love ya, Bowie," I tell him, and he lifts his chin happily, blinking his eyes, relishing the attention. "You're a good man," I say.

I brush my teeth, put on a jacket, and go for a walk. It's a cool morning, and there's little traffic on the downtown streets. Some people are walking to work; at least I imagine that's where they're headed. People—well-dressed and polished for the day—carrying brief cases and huge cups of coffee are going someplace to help make the world run like it does.

On Bagot Street, I take a right, walk two more blocks, and there it is: an old three-story, grey-brick building. It looks like someone's house, really. The words Limestone Mental Health Centre are etched on a sign to the left of the front doors.

I head up the front steps and have to ring a doorbell, because the doors are locked. A handwritten sign taped to the glass says: PLEASE RING DOORBELL. Then beneath that, almost as an afterthought, someone has written: ANYTIME. I don't hesitate. I ring the doorbell and think about how I'll introduce myself. "Hi. My name's Finny. I'd like to volunteer."

Sounds good to me: the simpler, the better.

~~~~~~

Jonah has grass stains on his jeans—one on the right knee and another larger one in the rear. "What happened to you?" I ask him.

A school bus pulls out of the parking lot and Jonah waves at the driver, a petite lady with short, feathered hair. She grins and trills her fingers at him.

"Football," Jonah says, as if that's explanation enough.

We head down the sidewalk. Jonah avoids stepping on the cracks, which makes me smile. His black-and-yellow knapsack is huge. He looks ready to climb a mountain.

Certain days now I walk him home from school. When Kathleen's working, typically, or when she has errands to run or needs to nap before work. Jonah's school bus drops him three blocks from his house. But they're busy streets, where he and his mother live. So when I offered to walk him home, Kathleen was happy to say yes.

"Did you get gang tackled or something?" I say.

"What?"

"Tackled by a whole bunch of guys," I explain.

"I got *creamed*," he says. "By a *girl!* Samantha Bigsby. She's gigantic. She's in grade six but she looks like she could be in high school."

"I played football in high school," I say. An older boy on a yellow skateboard rambles on by us, noisily, scraping cement, kicking up dust. "I was a place-kicker and a punter."
~~~~~~

"So you never got to tackle anyone?"

"I did on kickoffs and punts," I say.

"Oh," Jonah says, disappointed.

"But I wasn't very good at tackling. Mostly I tried not to get creamed myself. I could kick the hell out of a football, though."

Jonah ponders this. His lips looked chapped. I make a mental note to tell Kathleen later on.

"What I like is instrumental music," Jonah tells me. "I play the clarinet. Cleaning it's gross." He looks up at me, sticks out his tongue and puts a finger in his open mouth, as if gagging himself. "But I like playing it. Right now we're learning 'Let's All Sing Like The Birdies Sing.' It's hard."

"I don't know that one," I say.

"Oh. Well, it goes like this," Jonah tells me, and he whistles a sweet little melody.

I shake my head. "Nope. Don't know it. But I can't even whistle," I say.

Jonah looks shocked. "Really? I thought everybody could whistle."

"Well, not me."

"Try whistling this," Jonah tells me, and he purses his lips together, his chin dips, and he whistles a snippet of the song again. His whistling is clear and confident and tuneful. He's a natural.

I smile and laugh. I'm also excited. *Try Whistling This* is the title of a gorgeous Neil Finn record—his first solo effort, after Crowded House disbanded. It's one of my favourite albums. I'm so titillated by this coincidence, I want to tell Jonah all about it. But now he's looking up at me expectantly. "Now you try," he says.

So I try. And I fail miserably. I'm horribly off key. Jonah laughs and laughs. He slaps his pant leg, even. "Ha! You're *awful*," he says, and it seems like he'll never stop laughing.

~~~~~~

For the first time, Kathleen is coming over to my place. I'm nervous. What if she thinks it's ridiculous? With all the arcade games and lava lamps, blinking neon signs and pop art furniture? But at least the place is tidy; the gals from Molly Maid cleaned the apartment to a gleaming shine just this morning.

Still, when I buzz her in, I get butterflies. And then when she finally steps inside, after a hug and a kiss, I all but hold my breath.

"Oh my," she says. She looks up at the high, barrel ceilings and the loft and the sloped skylights, then down again—at everything else. "This is ... quite a place."

"Is that good or bad?" I say.

"Are you kidding?" she laughs. She smiles at me playfully, like I've been keeping a big juicy secret from her and have only now spilled the beans. "It's absolutely *beautiful!* I love it. Look at your kitchen! And that loft is gorgeous—and all the limestone and light." Her head swivels, this way, that way. "Where did you get all this funky furniture?" she asks. "Is that an old Davenport?"

"Yes. It's my writing desk."

"I love it!"

After that—after the initial shock and awe—Kathleen makes herself at home. I get us each a Heineken and we flake out on an open spot on the hardwood floor and play Scrabble. A Nina Simone record (Kathleen's choice) plays scratchily overhead, while we munch on dill pickle chips and eye up our tiles.

The first game, Kathleen whoops me. It's not even close.
~~~~~~

("And you have a degree in English Literature," she teases. "Tisk-tisk.") The second game is closer, but she beats me again. ("This is too easy," she says.) And then finally, I win the third game, but barely. ("I handed it to you," Kathleen tells me.)

"Show me the loft," she says.

"Sure."

We head up. She's impressed. "It has a cottage-y sort of feeling," she says. "You know?"

"I do. That was the idea."

She says, "Like this"—holding up an ornamental peacock candle holder—"This I'd expect to find only at a cottage."

"I can't remember where that came from."

"How in the world did you get a king-sized bed up that skinny old staircase?" she asks, her eyebrows forming a V.

"I didn't. Movers did," I say.

"Aaah." She sits on the bed. Bounces up and down, measuring up the mattress, I suppose. Then she smiles at me, all rascally, sexily, gesturing in slow motion with her index finger for me to come closer. I sit down next to her and she kisses me. And I kiss her back. We fall back, then roll over, still kissing and kissing. We're like high school kids.

We make love. And it's fabulous and intimate. Kathleen's hair is a lovely mess, and I get to laughing. "Well, you should see *your* hair," she says, laughing as well. "Who cuts this bee's nest, anyway? And what do they use: a hacksaw? Pruning sheers?"

"I cut it myself," I say. She's tickling me now, so I'm giggling as I talk. "Mostly. I only go to the barber's for a shave ... once ... in a blue moon. Stop that!"

Later, we take separate showers, and then Kathleen roots through my closet and picks out a white button-down shirt and puts it on. She looks incredibly sexy in my shirt and a pair of socks that remind me of a rainbow. "That's a good look for you," I say.

"Thanks," Kathleen says, but then she puts on the rest of her outfit, and I get dressed as well.

"Let's go to Fitzgerald's," I say.

"Sure."

"Fiona's playing."

"Oh, great," Kathleen says. "I've been dying to meet her. And hear her music."

But this worries me. Three nights ago, Fiona phoned me and she was very upset. She began to cry. Then she told me she'd seen Layton at a coffee shop with another woman and that they were obviously out on a date. "Can you come over?" she'd asked me, sniffling, blowing her nose, weeping. But I was halfway out the door; I'd promised to go watch Jonah play softball. I told Fiona as much. And then she'd screamed, "Fine! I'll just sit here and bawl my eyes out and climb the walls! Run along to your ready-made family now!"

"It's not like that," I'd said, but already she'd slammed the phone down and hung up.

The next day I went to the book shop and talked to her. She seemed fine, acted it like it had never happened. So I'd left it at that.

I let Kathleen choose a hat for me. She picks a grey tweed newsboy and puts it on me, tugging it down over my eyes. "I've a cool hat, see," she says, impersonating an actress from a '30s movie. "So come score a paper off me, two bits is all. Read all about it, Mac!"

Her acting is dead on. I laugh so hard I fall over onto my bed, holding my aching belly.

My belly is still a little sore when we get to Fitzgerald's. And Kathleen's all post-coital giddy. "I want a Caesar. Or no, a

Mojito," she says. "What's in a Tom Collins? Have you ever had a Tom Collins?"

"Nope."

"Or Sex-On-The-Beach. What's that all about?"

"Something fruity, I think. But hardcore. I don't know."

"Hmm. You know what, I'll just have a pint of beer."

It's busy. Every booth is taken, so we stand at the bar. From Jennifer, one of the weekend bartenders, I order our drinks: two pints of Keith's. We can hear Fiona playing the opening chords of a song, but we can't see her very well. We shuffle down near the end of the bar for a better view. And there's Fiona on stage, in a simple pink sweater, sitting posture-perfect behind her electric piano, her mousy black hair shining beneath a single yellow spotlight. Her head is bowed, her eyes closed. It's a lovely ballad, she's playing, a dark, wandering song about loneliness called "Forgotten Soldier." The crowd is fairly quiet as Fiona sings:

> *No one knows my face*
> *My map is smudged and torn*
> *I'm hunting every place*
> *Where you tell me I was born*

She belts out the last line, punching home the word *born*. And there's a murmur in the crowd—people taking notice. More faces turn toward the stage as Fiona's voice climbs higher, her lips close to the microphone:

> *And people take me in*
> *At every station of the cross*
> *They say I'm bathed of sin*
> *Only by the things I've lost*

Her voice cracks purposefully on the word *lost*. I've heard her play this song fifty times, at least; she played it for me the day after she'd written it, saying, "I want the chords to be dark and low and guttural. So you can feel it in your gut. Like you've been sucker punched."

Kathleen turns to me and whispers in my ear: "She's magnificent."

I nod. She truly is. Mesmerizing, too.

When she finishes the song, there is a loud round of applause and some whistles as well. Fiona bows her head, blushing, blinking her eyelashes nervously, rarely meeting anyone's glance. She is silent. She never says, "Thank you."

I feel a pang of sad nostalgia. I sip my beer but I can't shake the feeling. I need to leave. Maybe I've seen too many of these shows. Heard too many depressing songs about the same things: loss, loneliness, rejection, death, sadness. They can smother you, even though the music may sound lovely and Fiona's voice may be a wonderful instrument in itself. And maybe I feel bad for Fiona—for a hundred different reasons, but mainly because she's stuck in a dark, suffocating place and I don't want to be anywhere near it. Whatever it is, I need to get out of here. "I need some fresh air," I tell Kathleen.

"Are you okay?" she says.

"I don't know."

We make our way through a maze of blurry faces and leather jackets, then head out the side door. In the courtyard, I walk over to a lamp post and steady myself against it. I drink down half my beer like it's milk.

"What is it?" Kathleen asks me, rubbing my back.

"I just felt a little ... claustrophobic." I set my pint glass on the ground. Kneeling, I take in a few slow, deep breaths. Then I slowly stand again. Kathleen's looking at me with genuine concern. She gives me space to breathe. And I love that about her.

"I can't listen to those songs anymore," I say, and let out a long, slow, rapturous sigh of relief, like a frightened flyer might do after a safe landing. "Do you wanna go for a walk?" I ask Kathleen.

She smiles kindly, and says, "Sure."

~~~~~~

I make a great breakfast, and I'm just about to bite into the most delicious scrambled egg sandwich, when the phone rings. I sigh. Set the sandwich on a plate. Answer the phone.

"Mr. McKee?" says a man with a very deep voice. I wonder if this is a joke. The Caller I.D. on my phone says: Unknown Caller, Private Number.

"Yes."

"This is Dr. Gideon calling from Kingston Mercy Hospital," he says. "We have a patient in our care, a Miss Fiona Walters, who has listed you as her emergency contact."

Something takes a nose dive in my stomach. I sit down. "Okay?" I say. My hands begin to tingle.

"There's no cause to be alarmed," he says. "But we needed to contact you—"

"What happened? What is it?" I say, heaving the words and gulping for air.

"Well, she's fine now and resting," he says, gently, clearly practiced in bedside manner. "She was brought into the Emergency Department earlier this morning by ambulance, having overdosed on a number of medications."
~~~~~~

"*Overdosed?*"

"She was unconscious for a short time, but regained consciousness shortly after being admitted—"

"She tried to *kill herself?*" I say. The words seem to just come on their own.

The doctor clears his throat. "May I suggest, Mr. McKee, that you come to the hospital so that I can speak to you in person?"

"Oh, well ... certainly," I say. "Just tell me where to go. I'm familiar with the hospital."

"Come to the Emergency Room admitting desk and identify yourself. I'll be right here to meet you."

I hang up the phone. Then call a taxi. I flip off my slippers and put on a pair of sneakers, grab my keys and wallet, then head out the door.

~~~~~~

Dr. Gideon takes me into a small room with couches and chairs and lamps—it's like someone's tiny living room, with yellowing walls and fluorescent lighting and way too many magazines. I sit in a chair, leaning forward, scratching my scalp, wringing my hands. Dr. Gideon, a tall, thin, balding man, mid-forties, sits on the sofa next to me, holding a clipboard and a file folder.

He tells me Fiona is okay. In no physical danger. Her stomach's been pumped. She is resting and sore but in excellent hands. Since this was technically a suicide attempt, the doctor informs me, Fiona is being kept under close supervision by a number of nurses (Kathleen is working, I think, but not on this floor, and what time is it, anyway?) and will be seen by a psychiatrist shortly.

My mind is a swirling mess. I comb my hands through my
~~~~~~

hair and say, "Okay ... so, what's ... so what exactly happened?" He can see that I'm anxious. Then I tell him, "Dr. Gideon, I actually suffer from anxiety disorder so I'm feeling rather ... um ... antsy at the moment ... can you just, you know, be straight with me?"

So he relaxes a little, and puts the file folder and clipboard next to him on the sofa, and tells me what he knows: a toxicology report shows that Fiona ingested a number of medications. He lists them off, but the names are clinical-sounding and mean nothing to me. I don't know what they are. She'd left some music playing loudly in her apartment, he tells me, and a neighbour, a Mrs. Elmsley (who? I can't think of—oh yes, an elderly lady lives in the same apartment complex as Fiona, across the hall—she makes Fiona cookies—the walls are paper thin) knocked on Fiona's door to complain, found the door open, saw Fiona passed out on the floor, and called 911. The call was received at 4:30 A.M. Paramedics arrived at Fiona's apartment within fifteen minutes, and she was admitted to the hospital at 4:55 A.M.

I lean back in the chair and shake my head. "She tried to kill herself," I say, staring at the little holes in the ceiling tiles. "I knew this would happen one day."

And I'm angry. Though I don't know why. I guess because she didn't call me—and that she did this, *at all*. Also, I feel guilty. Angry at myself. I should have paid more attention to her recently when I knew she wanted it. Even though part of the reason I didn't give her as much attention as she likely wanted was to distance myself from her. And that makes me feel even more guilty.

Dr. Gideon says, "Frankly, if she really wanted to kill herself, she would have. Most people who truly want to commit suicide are successful. No, this was clearly an attempt to gain attention. A cry for help, if you will. And when Dr. Warner gets here—he's the psychiatrist on call—well, he'll have a good talk with her and evaluate the situation."

~~~~~~

I'm allowed to wait in the room where I met with Dr. Gideon. I wait and wait and wait. Pretty much empty out the water cooler in the corner. Flip through a few magazines, mostly just looking at the pictures. Then I buy a Coke from a vending machine in the actual waiting room and nervously smoke several cigarettes outside in the parking lot. It's a sunny day in May. Lots of traffic swishes by. I think maybe I should call someone, but who? Fiona hasn't talked to her parents in years, not since she left home the very day she turned eighteen. Besides, would they even care now? And how would I find them? Last Fiona spoke of them was, oh, five years ago, maybe. She'd told me that they might have moved to the States. But that was all she told me. I have no idea where she got her information. She didn't want to talk about it, so I didn't ask her any questions.

After I've used the washroom for the fifth time, an older gentleman in a shirt and tie and a white lab coat approaches me.

"Mr. McKee?" he says

"Dr. Warner?"

He smiles and extends his hand. I shake it, not so firmly. I'm tired and achy from sitting around so long.

"Yes," he says, all business. "Please follow me."

"Oh ... okay."

He walks me through the Emergency Room, which smells like rust and ammonia and the dentist's office, then down a
~~~~~~

short hallway. We come to stand outside a room with a pebbled glass window which reads "PRIVATE"—and Dr. Warner turns and faces me. "You're a friend of Fiona's," he says. It's not a question.

"Yes. A lifelong friend."

"Dr. Gideon explained the situation to you." Again, not a question.

"He did," I say. "How is she?"

"Well, she's just fine," he says, in a more friendly tone. "I've evaluated her and don't believe she's a threat to herself or anyone else. Her last medical records are from seven years ago, however, so I'm a bit sketchy on her past and wanted to ask you just a few questions."

"Sure," I say. "Okay."

"Then after that," he tells me, "you can talk to her, and after Dr. Gideon checks her over again and she signs a few standard forms, she'll be free to go home."

"I understand," I assure him, perhaps a bit abruptly.

Then he's all business again. He asks me if Fiona's had any history of mental illness. I tell him that she's been prone to mood swings most of her life, but that's about it. Any history of mental illness in her family that I know of? No, I respond, though Fiona's mother was rather ... unstable. She was abusive, I add. Physically and emotionally.

"All right," he says, seemingly satisfied.

"And she's always been emotionally fragile," I offer. "Fiona, I mean."

The doctor nods his head. "All right. Thank you for your help," he says, and pats me on the shoulder. "You can see her now." And he gestures to the door behind him, which I open only when he's halfway down the hall.

Fiona's lying in a hospital bed below some frightening looking X-Ray equipment. A woman in nursing scrubs is sitting in a green plastic chair next to her. She has neat, short hair. A name tag. Sensible sneakers. She gets up when she sees me, smiles. "I'll be right outside if you need me," she says.

"Thank you," I say.

She quietly shuts the door behind her.

Fiona is clothed in a flimsy green hospital gown, and she has white bracelets with typing on them on each wrist. Her face is streaked with mascara. There's a bandage on her left arm just below her elbow and a yellow-purple bruise on her left temple. *She must have fallen and hit her head,* I think. And picturing that makes me sad. I feel sorry for her. I'm relieved she's okay. I'm not really angry anymore.

"Hi," I say, but it's barely audible. I clear my throat and try again. "Hi. How are you feeling?"

She looks at me. She looks afraid, ashamed, tired, on the verge of tears. "Been better," she says.

I take a seat where the nurse had been sitting. Fiona looks away from me, at some spot on the wall.

"Fee, listen," I say. "I don't know why you did this, but I'd like to understand."

She sniffles. Puts a hand over her mouth. "I was just born," she says quietly. "That's all. I was born. I did nothing wrong. What did I do to make her hate me so much? I don't understand." And now she begins to cry, short little sobs, and I reach out and take her left hand in both of mine.

"I don't know," I tell her. "I honestly don't. But I'm beginning to think that there are just evil people in the world, and who knows why? I don't, but there just are—people who wish you ill, who want to harm you ... and for no good reason in the world, seemingly."

She squeezes my hand and closes her eyes tightly. I wipe the tears from her cheeks with the sleeve of my sweater.

"You know, Einstein once said—and I have this memorized, believe it or not, with my feeble memory—he said:

'The world is not dangerous because of those who do harm but because of those who look at it without doing anything.' And I think he may have been right, Fee."

Fiona clears her throat. Sounds like she needs to spit. She swallows. Looks at me with wounded eyes. "How so?" she says in a scratchy voice.

I take a deep breath and a firmer grip on her hand. "I am your friend, Fee, and I will always love you," I say, summoning courage from someplace deep within me. "And you know that; I know you do ... But I don't think I can be here for you like you need me to be here for you. I just can't do it anymore. Life moves forward. I'm changing. I feel like I'm becoming a better person, I really do. And I think that what you need right now is professional help. I think you need to talk about your past. About your mother. I think you need to get it all out of you and face it. Really deal with it. With a professional. But I'm not a professional. I can't help you with that. I think it's time you did something for yourself. Don't not do anything. You know?"

I was expecting her to pull her hand away, or snap at me, but instead she nods her head, ever so slightly. "I do," she says. "I'm tired of feeling ... afraid—*all the time*."

"Me too, sweetie."

"I'm tired of feeling *abandoned*," Fiona says. "I'm sick of myself. My whole body aches from thinking too much ... from trying too hard. From trying to please everyone." She coughs. Then she says, "Finny, am I a bad person? I feel like ...."

"No," I tell her firmly. "You're not a bad person. You're sweet and funny and generous and kind and—"

She laughs, spittle flying off her lips. "Enough," she says. And the corners of her mouth turn up a little. She looks oddly, tiredly at peace. Resigned. "I may have hit bottom but I'm not dead," she says.

We both smile at that. And I think to myself: Fiona might

be okay. This might have been a good thing for her, hitting bottom.

"Remember Ms. Plumb?" I ask her.

"What?" she says, confused. Then, "Oh, yes. I do. Why? Is she dead?"

I laugh. "No. Well, I don't know actually. Maybe. But I was just thinking about something she once said to me. She said, 'You can't just walk between the rain drops.' And you know ... she was bang on, I think. None of us can."

Fiona lets out a laugh. "*Ta*," it sounds like. "I might be hung over," she says, "but that sounds about right."

"Hung over?"

"Vodka," Fiona moans. "I poured a mickey of vodka into my blender. Then I went to my medicine cabinet and grabbed some pill bottles. All I had were aspirins and birth control pills. I looked for something else, but all there was was some old cough syrup. So then I put it all in the blender with some strawberry ice cream."

"A Suicide Smoothie," I say.

She laughs, and this time it's a good old sniffle-laugh. "It actually didn't taste so bad," she says.

Acknowledgments

Top thanks to my editor, the ever-studious Erin Daley, whose "fresh eyes" and constant encouragement made completing this book possible. She also helped keep me relatively sane throughout the process, and how can you repay someone for that?

For their opinions, insights, and careful reading of portions of this book, I greatly appreciate the help I received from: Jason Heroux, Stuart Ross, Julia Asselstine, Carlos Neves, and Liam McFadden.

For their kind (and free) support and guidance to a thirty-something writer shaking, sometimes literally, in his boots, I would like to thank Tish Cohen and Philip Beard, both excellent writers and goodhearted folks.

Heartfelt thanks to five excellent teachers—and friends—who supported, inspired and encouraged me over the years: Mr. O'Brien, Mr. Kellway, and Professors Joe Callahan, Scott Whalen and Robert Washburn.

I would also like to thank the Ontario Arts Council for a Writers' Works In Progress Grant received during work on *The Nothing Waltz*. Yours was the best mail I have ever received!

I also need to thank some friends who had faith in me when mine faltered: Stephen Scanlon, Bruce Urquhart, Ana Cavacas, Ian Houghton, Angela Meharg, Christine Robertson, Paul Law, Shirley Piersma, Nicole Hill, and the Daley family: Patricia,

Kevin and Mark. Thank you as well to Dr. Francis Jarrett, and he knows why.

For his hard work, kindness and patience, sincere thanks to Tai / Richard M. Grove.

Finally, for their love and support, I would like to thank my family: Mom, Dad, my sister Liz, her husband John, and my four thoughtful and inspiring nephews: Jacob, Christopher, Jora, and Ben. And for being perhaps my biggest fan over the years, thank you Aunt Yvette.

About the Author

John Pigeau was born in North Bay, Ontario and now lives and writes in Kingston, Ontario. As a journalist and poet, he has been published in numerous literary magazines, newspapers, and anthologies. *The Nothing Waltz* is his first novel.

Educated at Queen's University in English Literature and at Loyalist College in Print Journalism, John has also lived in London, Belleville, and the lovely village of Westport. In the journalistic trenches, he has been a desker, reporter, features writer, photographer, music critic, film reviewer, advertising salesman, and a newspaper editor. He is currently editing his first book of poetry, *Get Brave*, and working on his second novel, *Tether*.

Books in the North Shore Series

Find full information at
– http://www.HiddenBrookPress.com/b-NShore.html

First set of five books

— M.E. Csamer – Kingston – *A Month Without Snow*
   – Prose – ISBN – 978-1-897475-87-2
— Elizabeth Greene – Kingston – *The Iron Shoes*
   – Poetry – ISBN – 978-1-897475-76-6
— Richard Grove – Brighton – *A Family Reunion*
   – Prose – ISBN – 978-1-897475-90-2
— R.D. Roy – Trenton – *A Pre emptive Kindness*
   – Prose – ISBN – 978-1-897475-80-3
— Eric Winter – Cobourg – *The Man In The Hat*
   – Poetry – ISBN – 978-1-897475-77-3

Second set of five books

— Janet Richards – Belleville – *Glass Skin*
   – Poetry – ISBN – 978-1-897475-01-0
— R.D. Roy – Trenton – *Three Cities*
   – Poetry – ISBN – 978-1-897475-96-4
— Wayne Schlepp – Cobourg – *The Darker Edges of the Sky*
   – Poetry – ISBN – 978-1-897475-99-5
— Benjamin Sheedy – Kingston – *A Centre in Which They Breed*
   – Poetry – ISBN – 978-1-897475-98-8
— Patricia Stone – Peterborough – All Things Considered
   – Prose – ISBN – 978-1-897475-04-1

Third set of five books

— Mark Clement – Cobourg – *Island In the Shadow*
  – Poetry – ISBN – 978-1-897475-08-9
— Anthony Donnelly – Brighton – *Fishbowl Fridays*
  – Prose – ISBN – 978-1-897475-02-7
— Chris Faiers – Marmora – *ZenRiver Poems & Haibun*
  – Poetry – ISBN – 978-1-897475-25-6
— Shane Joseph – Cobourg – *Fringe Dwellers* Second Edition
  – Prose – ISBN – 978-1-897475-44-7
— Deborah Panko – Cobourg – *Somewhat Elsewhere*
  – Poetry – ISBN – 978-1-897475-13-3

Forth set of five books

— Diane Dawber – Bath – *Driving, Braking and Getting out to Walk*
  – Poetry – ISBN – 978-1-897475-40-9
— Patric Gray – Port Hope – *This Grace of Light*
  – Poetry – ISBN – 978-1-897475-34-8
— John Pigeau – Kingston – *The Nothing Waltz*
  – Prose – ISBN – 978-1-897475-37-9
— Mike Johnston – Cobourg – *Reflections Around the Sun*
  – Poetry – ISBN – 978-1-897475-38-6
— Kathryn MacDonald – Shannonville – *Calla & Édourd*
  – Prose – ISBN – 978-1-897475-39-3

Fifth set of three books

— Tara Kainer – Kingston - *When I Think On Your Lives*
  – Poetry– ISBN – 978-1-897475-68-3

— Morgan Wade – Kingston – *The Last Stoic*
  – Novel – ISBN – 978-1-897475-63-8

— Kathryn MacDonald – Shannonville – *A Breeze You Whisper*
  – Poetry – ISBN – 978-1-897475-66-9

Single Anthology

Changing Ways is a book of prose by Cobourg area authors including: Jean Edgar Benitz, Patricia Calder, Fran O'Hara Campbell, Leonard D'Agostino, Shane Joseph, Brian Mullally. Editor: Jacob Hogeterp
  – Prose — ISBN – 978-1-897475-22-5

9 781897 475379